DOWN-BEAT KILL

Peter Chambers

CHIVERS
THORNDIKE

This Large Print book is published by BBC Audiobooks Ltd, Bath, England and by Thorndike Press®, Waterville, Maine, USA.

Published in 2005 in the U.K. by arrangement with the Author.

Published in 2005 in the U.S. by arrangement with Peter Chambers.

U.K. Hardcover   ISBN 1–4056–3437–5 (Chivers Large Print)
U.K. Softcover   ISBN 1–4056–3438–3 (Camden Large Print)
U.S. Softcover   ISBN 0–7862–8013–1 (British Favorites)

The text of this Large Print edition is unabridged.
Other aspects of the book may vary from the original edition.

Set in 16 pt. New Times Roman.

Printed in Great Britain on acid-free paper.

British Library Cataloguing in Publication Data available

Library of Congress Cataloging-in-Publication Data

Chambers, Peter, 1924–
    Down-beat kill / by Peter Chambers.
        p.   cm.
    "Thorndike Press large print British favorites."—T.p. verso.
    ISBN 0–7862–8013–1 (lg. print : sc : alk. paper)
    1. Private investigators—Fiction. 2. Television broadcasting—
Fiction. 3. Large type books. I. Title.
PR6066.H463D69 2005
823'.914—dc22   2005017570

NEWSFLASH

. . . and here is news of a sensational bomb explosion which tonight ended the star-studded career of top disc jockey Donny Jingle. Less than eight minutes ago the star of television's Double Dee Jay Show was killed instantly as his car blew up outside the A.I.C.T. building here in Monkton City. Police were on the scene as your reporter . . .

*   *   *

Lights were discreetly low on the dance floor as the small orchestra swung smoothly into *Night and Day*. The tall man with the prematurely grey hair smiled down at the attractive brunette in his arms. They made a pleasing sight as they moved easily to the music. A black-coated waiter threaded his way to the side of the floor. When the couple came close he tapped the man respectfully on the shoulder and whispered in his ear. The grey-haired man frowned and looked past the waiter to the curtained awning, where another man stood, waiting. A man in a police uniform.

*   *   *

The tall man sipped slowly at his drink, while

1

the man at the other side of the table seemed half-asleep. The drinker was humming softly to a tune on the radio. Then he stopped humming and started listening. He got up, spoke quickly to his sleepy companion and left the restaurant.

*   *   *

The girl was getting ready to go out. A silver lamé evening gown lay across a chair-back. She was unbuttoning a check lumberjack shirt, cherry hair tumbling over her forehead as she bent. Suddenly she stopped, moved to the radio in the corner, and turned it up loud. For a moment she went white, then she sat heavily in a chair, and reached for the bottle which stood expectantly on a low table by her side.

*   *   *

A fat, elderly man was busy scraping out a cherrywood pipe. He paused as the harsh radio voice droned into the hushed atmosphere of his elegant office. Then he looked up at the two men who waited expectantly at the other side of his desk.

'Are they all on their way?'

'We're working on it, sir,' one of them assured him. The fat man stabbed his pipe towards the radio. 'You heard that. Get something done about it.'

2

*   *   *

The bartender kept a watchful eye on the middle-aged woman who sat propped up at the end of the bar. There was a lost sadness on her face which was not calculated to cheer up the other customers. Two men were sitting next to her, chattering away. Without warning she grabbed one by the arm. 'What'd you say? Who's dead?'

'Donny Jingle, the tee-vee star,' he grumbled. 'Hey, lay offa my arm, huh?'

She didn't seem to hear. Still hanging on to his coat, she began to laugh. Wild, uncontrollable spasms of laughter. Not balanced laughter, but with something almost maniacal about it.

Two or three people looked round uncomfortably. The bartender sighed, and made up his mind.

She was still laughing as he pushed her out into the night.

*   *   *

A white convertible pulled in to the side of the road. The driver, a big cheery-looking man, sat listening intently to the car-radio. His face was thoughtful. Then, as the reader passed to the next item, the driver smiled suddenly, a great wide smile that lit up his eyes. Checking back

3

over his shoulder he eased the convertible round in a wide arc and headed back towards the bright-lit city. He was singing.

CHAPTER ONE

Amalgamated Inter-coastal Television was tucked modestly inside fourteen floors of steel, concrete and glass. Just so you wouldn't overlook the place, the famous station identification A-I-C-T was splashed across the front of the building in letters sixteen feet high. I left the Chev in the lot at the side marked 'Visitors' and approached the main entrance on foot.

The doorman was dressed up like a general in some South American army. He would have been impressive enough in his underwear, a towering figure of around six feet six and with shoulders to match. In the purple uniform with scarlet pockets and epaulettes plus silver buttons he was a gorgeous sight. He looked me over quickly as I approached, spotted a stranger and decided on the treatment.

'Good afternoon,' was his greeting. He didn't open a door. I told him good afternoon and pushed open the nearest of the all-glass entrance doors. The doorman was an unfailing judge of visitors, otherwise he wouldn't have the job. I didn't rate a salute or the door bit. On the other hand I didn't look poor enough to ignore entirely. So he played it safe, just in case I might get to rate with A.I.C.T. and bear him in mind. Inside I walked on shining black marble across to a white counter of the same material about thirty feet in length.

Behind it four girls were spaced out evenly, each at a small pink desk with pink telephones. They were interchangeable, these four. All blondes, dressed in black silk blouses and white linen skirts. All beautiful, all groomed, all with the same expression of amused boredom. I leaned on the counter and the nearest one said:

'Good afternoon, sir. Can I help you?'

The voice was pleasant, impersonal, and a half-smile went with it.

'I'm here to see Donny Jingle. Four o'clock appointment. The name is Mark Preston.'

The pleasantness in the voice moved up three grades.

'Just one moment, Mr. Preston.'

She talked softly into one of her telephones. I leaned on the marble counter and wondered what Donny Jingle wanted with me. Maybe he'd found out I was one of the few people in the State of California who didn't watch his programme, and he was going to demand an explanation.

The receptionist finished her conversation, flashed me two rows of flawless white teeth and said warmly:

'You're to go up right away, Mr. Preston. The attendant will show you the way.'

Suddenly there was a teenage boy standing at my elbow, dressed like a Junior Officer in the doorman's army. He had nice teeth too, a curly dark-haired boy with an open face.

'Right this way, Mr. Preston.'

I thanked the blonde and followed the attendant to the elevator bank. A.I.C.T. evidently had a nice organisation, when they wanted to be nice. It flattered me, although I knew all the dressing was not because of who I was, but who I was going to see.

Inside the elevator the boy said:

'For every visitor I take up to Mr. Jingle I show about twenty back out the front entrance, Mr. Preston.'

'Really? Bill-collectors?'

He smiled politely.

'No, sir. Music publishers, song-pluggers, singers, musicians. They don't get off the ground floor without an appointment.'

'Then it's as well I left my saxophone home.'

He was still trying to decide whether that was a gag when the elevator stopped at twelve. We got out and he led me through two corridors till we came to a door with the legend

DOUBLE D-J
KEEP OUT

I expected the kid to open it. Instead he pressed a bell at the side. A man opened the door and looked us over.

'Mr. Mark Preston,' announced my escort.

7

'Appointment with Mr. Jingle, four o'clock.'

The man grunted and addressed me.

'Any identification, Mr. Preston?'

'Sure.'

I handed him the leather fold which has my P.I. licence and picture inside. He looked at the picture then again at me.

'This way, Mr. Preston.'

The kid melted away and I went with my new friend. I wondered where he fitted in, this broad-shouldered ugly man with the suspicious eyes. He led me through two smaller offices, busy with typewriters and telephones, and into a slightly larger room where a striking brunette sat behind a mahogany desk. If she had any work to do, there wasn't any of it in view. The black hair was swept back from the perfect oval of her face, accentuating the fine black lines of her pencilled eyebrows and giving prominence to high cheekbones. It was an intelligent face, which now regarded me with interest.

'You are Mr. Preston?'

I nodded.

'Thank you, Charlie.'

Charlie gave another of his grunts and went away. I hardly noticed. No man was going to look at Charlie or anybody else while this delectable dish was within range.

'I'm Nicola Hardin,' she informed me. 'Mr. Chisum will be right out.'

'And just who is Mr. Chisum?' I asked.

'He's assistant to Mr. Jingle,' she replied evenly. 'Takes care of a lot of business for him.'

'Uh huh. And you, Miss Hardin,' I kept on looking at her, 'You work for Chisum or Jingle?'

'I'm Mr. Jingle's personal secretary,' she said. 'Please sit down if you wish.'

She wore a sleeveless green blouse which buttoned up to the smooth column of her throat. It wasn't an eye-catcher, just a simple garment. But it wasn't the kind of simplicity you pick up in the bargain basement. The bracelet around her wrist hadn't come from a five and dime either. Miss Hardin seemed to be a gal who liked nice things. I thought idly it would be a pleasant experience to be included among the nice things for a spell. Before I got a chance to bring up the subject a man rushed into the room.

He was a couple of inches shorter than me, maybe five ten, but on the heavy side. Straggly fair hair was beginning to recede from the wrinkled forehead. I put him down as in his early thirties.

'Mr. Preston?' he asked anxiously.

'Yes. You're Mr. Chisum?'

We shook hands. His grip was dry and firm, but perfunctory.

'Please come into my office,' he jerked. 'Oh and Nicola—don't tell Mr. Jingle our visitor is here. Not yet.'

'Very well.'

He led me into a room leading off from Nicola Hardin's office, and sat me down in a hideous plastic chair. He didn't sit but paced up and down as he spoke.

'Well, er, Mr. Preston, you'll be wondering what this is all about, naturally.'

'Naturally.'

'Yes, well, er, let me tell you something about the set-up here. For a start, you hardly need me to tell you who Donny Jingle is, eh?'

He laughed, a short, nervous sound. I shook my head.

'Hardly. He gets enough publicity. He must be one of the top disc-jockeys in the business. Outside of that, I don't know anything about him at all.'

Chisum nodded, rubbing his hands together quickly.

'May as well tell you, Preston, I'm sticking my neck out bringing you into this. Donny doesn't think much of the idea, and as for Kingworth, well he doesn't even know.'

'Kingworth? Who is Mr. Kingworth?' I queried.

'Vance Kingworth?' It was obvious from the horrified tone that Chisum thought I should know about Kingworth. 'Why he's executive vice-president of the network. One of the top men. *The* top man as far as Double Dee Jay is concerned.'

He stopped pacing around, ran a hand

10

through the wispy hair, and sat down.

'I'm not handling this at all well,' he confessed. 'Let's start again. You see A.I.C.T. has three exec. v.p.'s—vice presidents that is. Each of them takes personal control of so much network business. One of the three is Kingworth.'

'And one of the Kingworth shows is the Double Dee Jay,' I finished.

'Yup. At least, partly. You see, Double Dee Jay started about three years back. At the time it was just one of twenty shows or more that Kingworth handled. But it caught, brother how it caught. It climbed up the ratings like a forest fire. Now it's one of the network's major features, and so naturally Kingworth has to give it more and more attention.'

'And you say he doesn't know about me?'

'That's right. Not yet. You see the show hinges on Donny Jingle. He's the star attraction, as the circus boys say. Without him we're dead. Me, Nicola, the gag boys, script writers, ad. men—a whole string of people. That's why we all have to take this seriously, even if Donny doesn't.'

I lit an Old Favourite. Chisum refused.

'I don't know much about this business,' I told him.

'Only what I see coming through the screen. Surely it can't be as bad as that? I mean there'd be plenty more work if this show folded, especially for people from such a well-known programme?'

He grinned then, a quick smile that made him look almost boyish.

'Brother, you really are from outside. It doesn't work that way at all. Sure it's a well-known programme. But when a major show dies, everybody in it suddenly finds he has leprosy. He has the jinx. Everybody contributes something to a show, even if it's only a little. If the show goes bust, it could have been anybody's fault. So you don't work. Not for a long time anyway.'

It made just the off beat kind of sense that rang true.

'Are you telling me the Double Dee Jay is about to go off the screen?'

'No, no, no,' he was horrified again. It was as though somebody had sworn in church.

'You oughtn't to say things like that,' he remonstrated. 'Around here that does not rate a laugh. No. It's something else. It's Donny.'

'Is he sick or what?'

Whatever it was I wished Chisum would get on with it. He certainly had a talent for the suspense angle.

'Well, all right.'

The fair man dived into a desk drawer, took out a piece of paper, tossed it across to me. When I got it the right way round I found it was network memo paper. At the top was the inscription of the company, and underneath that was printed 'Double D-J-Show outline.'

The pay-off was the show outline. It was a list of what I took to be song-titles, though I didn't recall a few of them. It read:

Music Man
I'll be Around
Any Time
Anywhere
In the Still of the Night
High Noon
Some Day I'll Find You
With These Hands
There'll be some Changes Made
The Music Stops
I'll be Glad when you're Dead you Rascal You.

I nodded.

'All right I got the message. What's it all about?'

Chisum did his hand-rubbing trick, again.

'You see we always have an outline for the show. Lots of requests come in, you know, and the girls in the office go through them, sort out the titles most frequently asked for, and that gives Donny something to work with. He starts off with maybe a basic list of fifty titles and we break it down till we have a programme.'

'And this is one of those lists?'

'No. Well, that is, it isn't a real list. But that's the way they look when they first come to Donny, for the first rough shots at the script

13

and so on. But that isn't a real one. Somebody got that up specially and slipped it on his desk.'

I looked at the list again.

'A gag, maybe? I hear you have one or two humorists on the network. This may be a very funny joke.'

'No joke. You don't play jokes like that on the big attraction. Not at A.I.C.T. you don't. Not if you ever want to work in television again. Besides that isn't the end of the story.'

I put the ghoul's request list back on the desk. A man put his head round the door. He didn't knock. The face was round and worried-looking, in spite of the big smile that threatened to split it in two.

'Say, Dave—oh sorry. This your congressman?'

He beamed at me in a way that plainly said nobody ever got mad with him. I found myself grinning back.

'I'm a little busy, Mo. Could it wait a few minutes?'

'Wait? Sure, it can wait. It isn't anything at all. Just some lousy little idea of mine for putting this fill-show up in the top ratings, that's all it is. Just the hottest idea anybody ever hatched around this morgue. Nothing more.'

Ruffled, the face withdrew and the door closed.

'Strong silent type,' I commented.

Chisum flashed the boyish grin briefly and

14

waved a hand.

'Take no notice of him. That's Mo Shoeman, our ad-man, kind of layout king for the show. He comes up with those brainstorms about forty times in an average day. That's his business and he's good at it. But he'll keep. Where was I?'

I looked around for somewhere to park the butt of my cigarette, located a plastic nymph with scooped-out feet and got rid of it.

'You were saying there was more to it than the song-titles.'

'Oh yeah. Nobody paid much attention to the dummy outline, Donny just laughed it off. Two days later somebody took a shot at him.'

And now I was listening.

'Where was this?'

'At his home. He was walking towards the house from the garage when there was a shot. It missed him by about four inches and finished up in the wall. He hit the ground fast but whoever it was didn't try again.'

'Was he using a silencer?'

'No. Donny said he heard it loud enough. Why?'

'That's why he didn't hang around. Once you make a noise like that you're just begging to be caught if you stick around to give it another try.'

Chisum looked at me with what might have been respect.

'Say I never thought of that.'

15

'Why should you? This isn't your kind of business. Did you notify the police?'

He shook his head firmly.

'Absolutely not, Donny said no, Kingworth said no. And they were right too. If word got around that we might be losing Donny Jingle we'd be as dead as the last election results.'

'I see. Have you told me the whole story now?'

'You haven't had the poison try yet,' he told me. 'Monday of this week we were working late. We do a radio request thing Mondays at eight o'clock. Afterwards we try to get a couple of hours start on the television programme for the following Saturday. That'd be this Saturday.'

He paused to see if I was still with him. I was.

'I sent out for some sandwiches. We were chewing away when Donny suddenly said he had a pain in his stomach. Nicola was there and she wasn't eating. She grabbed his sandwich, sniffed at it. Then she poured all the mustard in a glass mixed it up with water and made Donny drink it. He was ill as all hell, but it got the stuff out of him. We had the sandwich analysed quietly. There was enough strychnine in the filling to kill a horse.'

'What kind of sandwich?'

'Ham on rye. But Donny's a great one for flavour. He'll put ketchup and pickles on a boiled egg if he isn't stopped. So with all the

16

muck he'd smeared inside he couldn't taste the stuff.'

I jerked my head towards the door.

'Miss Hardin, you mentioned. How come she was so quick off the mark?'

'Nicola didn't laugh about this the way the rest of us did,' he tapped at the paper on his desk. 'She worried about it, said she was sure it meant trouble. Then when the shooting happened, we had to admit she was right. So she was kind of keyed up, waiting for trouble if you like. And they tell me a woman will always think of poison quicker'n a man.'

I had to agree with that.

'So now Mr. Jingle brings me in. Not the police, who might do some good, not a big outfit like the Pinkertons who could guard him all round the clock, but me. One solitary P.I., complete with wisecracks and bag of miracles. We're wasting each other's time, Mr. Chisum. I can't take the responsibility of pretending to guard a man twenty-four hours a day. From gunfire, poisoned food and lord knows what all. Go to the police.'

I started to get up, but he motioned anxiously for me to sit down again.

'You have this wrong. Now in the first place, I don't even know if I've done the right thing in bringing you here. Donny's sure to get mad.'

'Why? Does he want to die?'

'No, it isn't that. He just says he's not going to be scared by some sneaky character who hasn't the guts to get up where he can see him.'

Whatever I thought privately of his programme, I was beginning to have some respect for the big D.J.

'So how are you going to explain me to him?' I enquired.

Chisum nodded and looked even more worried.

'I know. That's what I keep asking myself. Well, might as well get it over with. C'mon, let's go talk with Donny.'

He heaved himself erect like a man who'd just heard the tumbril halt outside. Then he sighed mournfully and led me back into Nicola Hardin's office. She looked at us quizzically.

'What'd you do to him, Mr. Preston?'

I shrugged and followed the dejected Chisum through a large door behind the brunette's desk. One drawer was open. In it I caught a glint of metal. Metal that looked like the barrel of a revolver.

'Well, Donny,' said Chisum, suddenly cheerful. 'Here we are.'

CHAPTER TWO

Donny Jingle sat on a huge table covered with coloured diagrams. He looked just the way he did on the glass screen, thick dark brown hair,

18

heavy featured but still handsome. He seemed to be in pretty good shape, a well disciplined one hundred and ninety packed solidly into his five feet nine inches. His clothes were riotous. Rainbow-coloured Hawaiian shirt flapping outside yellow casual slacks, set off with purple canvas shoes. The bare arms were strong and muscular with curly black hair growing most of the way up. On the other side of the table sat the man who'd butted in on my conversation with Chisum, the worried-looking Mo Shoeman.

At our entrance, both looked round.

'Well, here we are,' reiterated Chisum.

'C'mon in Dave,' boomed Jingle. 'Tell this schnuck we can't use stuff like this on a family programme, huh?'

Before Chisum could utter, Jingle spoke again,

'I mean tell the guy, will ya? Here I got the whole family looking at me over there in Witchita, grandma, cousin Elsie the whole works. Suddenly six dames walk in wearing these outfits? Lissen—'

He noticed me for the first time.

'—Oh, the newsreel thing, yes? Be with ya in a minute. Well c'mon, Dave, tell him.'

I stood there privately trying to decide whether it was a good thing or a bad thing to be mistaken for a newsreel thing. The jury were still out when Chisum managed to stop the flow.

'This is Mark Preston, the private investigator I mentioned to you this morning.'

Having finally got it out the fleshy man's nerve seemed to evaporate, and he stood waiting meekly for the storm. Shoeman's eyes were threatening to pop out of his head as he sat staring, first at me, then Chisum, then Donny Jingle. The disc-jockey's eyes narrowed slightly, and now he looked at me properly.

'Say again,' he said softly.

'The private investigator. We talked about it this morning.'

Jingle snorted.

'We talked about it? We? You mean you talked about it. All I did was listen. And say no. I don't want any bodyguard. Now pay him and get him outa here.'

'No, Donny.'

To my surprise, Chisum stood his ground. I'd have given long odds he would have collapsed like a pack of cards. Instead, he spoke quite firmly.

'Whether you personally are afraid or not, I'm telling you I am. So's everybody else on the crew. You may be the big name around here, but these are our jobs as well as yours this lunatic is messing with. A whole parcel of people. Something has got to be done.'

It was evident that Chisum's resolution was a surprise to Jingle as well as me. He stared hard at the fair man. The marines landed in the unexpected form of Mo Shoeman.

'Say, Donny, now the man's here, I have kind of idea about this.'

Jingle stared at Chisum for a few more seconds then swung his head slowly to look at the speaker.

'Well now,' he said quietly, 'Suddenly you have an idea. Everybody in the joint is loaded with ideas about this, except me. Your last idea Mo, is right here,' he jabbed a thumb at the coloured layouts on his table, 'a real beauty. You want to turn a family show into a two-bit burlesque house. It gives me confidence, Mo. It makes me just naturally anxious to know how you're going to handle this other thing.'

He sat and waited. Shoeman gulped, one worried frown after another chasing across the seamed forehead, while the great wide smile remained undisturbed on the lower half of his face. It was an astonishing sight.

'Well say now, Donny, this is just a practice kick you know. Just batting it around. I was thinking you don't want a bodyguard, well O.K. It's out. After all it's you that's out in the storm in the cockleshell boat. So O.K., you don't want some heavy breathing down your neck all the time, O.K. he's out. Cops are out, too, everybody agrees about that. Just the same, there is something going on we don't much care about. So, if you don't want the man hanging on to your shirt all day why don't we go at it the other way round? Like why don't we hire the guy to research around some, try to find out something that'll maybe point a finger. That way he won't get under your feet, but he will be doing something about all this, and who knows, he could even come up with a seven-pound villain. I mean, don't get me wrong, Donny, I'm not telling you your business, just trying to find something for the guy to do now he's here.'

Jingle listened carefully.

'Sure, I know, Mo. You're just batting it around.'

Shoeman was nodding with delight when the sarcastic inflexion in Jingle's tone registered. Then he didn't look so happy. Chisum winked at him gratefully.

'What was the name again?'

Jingle was looking at me. It was so long since I'd said anything I expected a rusty squeak, but my voice sounded quite normal.

'Mark Preston.'

'I've heard it before,' he observed.

'Perhaps. Sometimes if the newspapers are trying to rile the police department they give me a play.'

Jingle smiled, the way he always did as he introduced the latest disc.

'I got you. You're the one put the arm on that call-girl set-up a while back. [*The Big Goodbye*]'

'Partly,' I acknowledged.

He chewed on his lower lip and looked at me a while longer.

'You think you can do anything here? I mean, without walking on the grass, that is? We got a big operation, people are interested in it. Some are interested in keeping it running, some are just looking for a chance to knock it. Which way, you're going to draw a lot of light if you start clubfooting around the network. What would you do?'

'First I'd ask for a job. You'd have to hire me as an extra man of some kind. That way I'd be just part of the background.'

'Then what?'

'Then I'd have to play it by ear. Listen, watch, ask a question if I could do it without making any noses twitch.'

'He could help me get down that pile of paper in the outer office, Donny—' began Chisum.

'You're interrupting when I'm talking to the man,' Jingle's cold voice cut him off. 'What do you figure to find out round here?'

I shrugged.

'This is one of your people doing all this, has to be. The phoney show outline was typed on official paper. Also it was set up in the same way as a real programme, so whoever did it knows what a real programme looks like. And that sandwich you got, that had to be fixed by somebody who knew you were going to eat it.'

'Yeah.'

Jingle breathed heavily.

'We've known all along it had to be somebody who's in touch. I've been trying to keep off that kind of thinking because I don't want to know it's true. But you're right. I'll think it over. But I won't have you or anybody else imagine I'm scared of this guy. I always take care of myself, and I'll go on doing it.'

'Sure, Donny,' agreed Chisum.

'You bet,' chimed Shoeman.

'Let me talk to this ball-team a while, do you mind? You can wait in Dave's office.'

I went out but not to Chisum's office. To do that I'd have to go past Nicola Hardin and I'm too set in my ways for that.

She still wasn't doing any work that I could see. When I stood beside her desk she looked up at me and this time I was close enough to see her eyes were hazel.

'Coach is having a bull session with the team,' I told her. 'Seemed a good time for us to get to know each other better. Do you smoke?'

'No thank you. I'm also not certain I wish to get to know you any better,' she responded coolly.

'Give me a chance to work on it. You could make a mistake, Miss Hardin. I might be that big thing you've been waiting for.'

I tapped an Old Favourite from the pack, made a mental note to get more when I left. As I lit it she said:

'Mr. Preston, there are one or two hard

economic facts you should consider. I'm expensive. I like nice things, going to the best places. Around here there are plenty of people who can provide these amenities. I make it my business not to know any other kind of people. Why should I? A girl has what she has, and it's up to her to do her best with it. I know what business you're in, and I haven't ever heard of anyone in that line joining the millionaires club. So it looks like no deal.'

She spoke quite matter-of-factly, a vest-pocket analysis of the economic situation in its relation to Nicola Hardin. I grinned.

'I could probably scrape up enough hard money to buy you one drink in the best surroundings. Let's make it the cocktail bar at Raoul's, six o'clock this evening. By your reckoning, one drink in there ought to break me, so if you have me pegged right you should be free for the rest of the evening by six fifteen.'

She smiled, a lazy smile that slid easily across the full red lips.

'I like to drink, especially at Raoul's. So long as you don't imagine I'll be so dizzy from your masculine charm that I'll be talked into spending the rest of the evening at some drive-in movie. I'll be there.'

Before I could say anything else Chisum came bounding out of Jingle's office.

'Oh, there you are. C'm in a minute. Excuse us, Nicola.'

Back in his own office, Chisum almost whooped.

'He goes for it. Boy, here I've been thinking he'd push me out of a window or something, bringing you here this way. But he goes for it.'

'Fine. What happens now?'

He sat down, rubbing his hands. It was evidently a favourite pastime with the man.

'Don't mind telling you, Preston, now you're in, I've been having a bad time over this. You see, Donny puts on this big act about not being scared and all, but a lot of it is a front for the crew. Since the poison thing, he's really only held back going to the police because Kingworth won't have it. Donny's jumpy all right. You'd recognise the signs if you knew him like I know him. Know what he's made me do these past days?'

I shook my head.

'Taste all his food before he eats?'

'No. He would have if he'd thought of it. No, at nights we're usually the last to leave, Donny and me. One or two things to button up, you know the way it goes. Well, he's making me leave by the brass exit every night. That's a special side door downstairs, only to be used by the big names. The big names include Donny Jingle but not Dave Chisum. Not ordinarily, that is. Well, we're much the same size except I'm a little taller. He's been getting me to leave in his coat and hat and drive off in his car. Donny is not a quiet dresser as you probably noticed, and his street clothes are just as noisy. So unless you were close enough for a good look you'd probably mistake me for him when I go out that side entrance.'

'Enough like him to take a shot at, for example,' I murmured.

'For example,' he agreed. 'Anyway that's the deal, and if you think I'm enjoying it you're crazy.'

I didn't think he was enjoying it one bit. To me he looked scared and I couldn't say I'd blame him. Bad enough to feel somebody's trying to kill you if it was on the level, but to act as decoy so somebody else wouldn't get killed made it just that much worse.

'Mind if I call you Dave?'

'Everybody else does.'

'Well tell me something, Dave. Why do it? Why not just tell your boss this job does not include acting as a moving target for some maniac with a gun?'

He snorted derisively.

'Because he'd give me the door that's why. Donny can be a very funny guy when he chooses. And if anybody doesn't co-operate with him, he chooses.'

'So you might lose the job. I imagine you could get another.'

He raised his eyes towards the ceiling in an expression of controlled patience.

'That's what you imagine, huh? You're not a

good imaginer.'

He waved an arm to include the whole of Double Dee Jay in his next remark. 'You know what makes this show so special? Donny Jingle. You know the magic ingredient that keeps all of us around here in an inflated income bracket? Donny Jingle. This is the original one-man band. Anybody else in the show can be replaced by the difficult process of lifting a telephone. It happened already a coupla times. You know my market value, my real value on an open market? A hundred a week. Maybe one ten if the boss liked my face. Know what I pick up here?'

I shook my head.

'Two fifty. Two hundred and fifty bucks a week. I'm not worth it. I'm worth just less than half. But I don't want half. I want those two and a half centuries just as long as I can keep 'em coming. Kabish?'

A very old dodge in any business, but the entertainment industry has brought it to a fine art. Take one perfectly ordinary guy and promote him. Promote him way over his value and let him get used to the feeling. Then squeeze, gently but continually. Finally there's nothing he won't do to hang on to that job. If Jingle said hop, Chisum would hop, and go on hopping.

'All right, you sold me. So you wear the overcoat. Now, when do I go to work?'

'You already started. You're a methods

man. You're going to study all the programmes on the network. Double Dee Jay is first.'

'Sounds great. What do I study?'

'The whole operation. You watch the routine, see how much time is wasted at rehearsals and so forth. Watch for extravagance with the sets and costumes. Find out what everybody does, what their real contribution is to the show, if anything.'

'O.K. It's a good front. With that story nobody's going to spend a lot of time asking me what I do. Who knows the truth?'

'You, me, Donny, Mo, Nicola,' Chisum counted on his fingers.

'And we'll have to tell Kingworth.'

He didn't look happy at the prospect. I asked him:

'Who will tell him? You?'

'No, sir, not me. Donny can do that,' he replied emphatically.

'Let's get to the hard part. What is the lowest figure you'll work for to keep the great D-J in one piece?'

I'd been wondering about that myself.

'Who pays? Jingle, the network, Kingworth?'

'The network pays. That by itself should bring the price down. Why it's nothing less than a privilege to work for A.I.C.T. An honour. How much?'

'A hundred a day. Plus all expenses.'

He let out a whoosh of breath and stared at

me.

'A hundred a day? Now come on. I was thinking of say around twenty-five.'

I smiled pleasantly.

'Really? I was thinking of exactly one hundred. Take it or leave it.'

He gritted his teeth together and thought about it. 'You're a thief. But O.K. But no expenses.'

At those prices I could afford to be generous.

'No expenses,' I agreed. 'And I start from today. Got a sheet of paper?'

He pulled a fresh sheet from a drawer and passed it across. I wrote:

'The Amalgamated Inter-Coastal Television Company engages Mark Preston, private investigator, starting today at a fee of one hundred dollars per day. No expenses will be paid and this agreement cannot be terminated unless three days' notice are given in writing to the said Mark Preston.'
Signed
Witnessed
Date

'Get it signed, will you, Dave? Kingworth would be best, but I'll settle for Donny Jingle if, and only if, Miss Hardin is the witness.'

He read quickly through what I'd written.

'Brother, how'd you ever keep out of

30

Quentin?' he wanted to know. 'Why this is plain daylight robbery.'

'Isn't it though? You made a mistake picking somebody who looks at the financial columns. I know what this benevolent society tucked under the pillow last year. A.I.C.T. could pay me a thousand a day for ten years, and still take the money out of the office loose cash-box.'

He shook his head and went away. I strolled across to the window and looked out.

Monkton City is still growing, and there aren't yet the same profusion of tall buildings as in other cities round about. From the twelfth floor of the A.I.C.T. building I could get a good view of most of the town. I liked it. I like to get up high now and then and look at what a fine clean town we have. The blue of the Pacific washed lazily into shore, breaking white, and looking almost fluffy from that distance. In my business it's a good thing to be reminded occasionally of how peaceful a city can look. Lower down I'd find the thugs and pimps and the rest of the human sewage. But from that window they didn't exist. I was busy watching a race among some small sailing boats when Chisum came back. He handed me the paper. It was signed by Jingle and witnessed by Nicola Hardin.

'Thanks, Dave. I'll get along now. Got a lot to do.'

'You'll what? You'd better get started on

31

your job here,' he remonstrated.

'Uh uh,' I shook my head. 'Wouldn't look good. Who ever heard of a new man arriving at five in the afternoon? No, tomorrow morning. Ten o'clock. Besides, I want to get started on the outside too, you know.'

'Yeah?' He was interested. 'What're you going to do exactly?'

I wagged my head slowly from side to side.

'Sorry, Dave. From now on, I don't tell you what I'm doing. Only Jingle. Everybody else is on the other side as far as I'm concerned.'

'Me? You're nuts. Why, it was me brought you down here.'

'Sorry, Dave. Tomorrow morning I'll report for work. So long.'

CHAPTER THREE

When I got back to my own office Miss Digby seemed surprised to see me.

'Why, Mr. Preston, I hardly expected to see you back this late.'

Florence Digby does not approve of me. She does not like my lack of business routine, my behaviour, the people I know. All round I could not single out one aspect of my existence which came in for the warm glow of Miss Digby's blessing. Maybe it's a good thing. We certainly complement one another. Any

32

dignity or system there is about my business is due to her tireless campaign to make a respected community figure out of me. Florence must be in her middle forties now, attractive still in her well-tailored, aloof way. One of the great puzzles in my life has always been to wonder why nobody ever married the girl. She must have been a knockout in her earlier years. But with Miss Digby, the mystery would remain. There are things I would dare and things I wouldn't. Asking my highly-efficient secretary about her private life fell solidly into the second category.

'Miss Digby, I need Sam Thompson in a hurry, I want him here in the office just as fast as possible. Can you find him?'

'Of course,' she replied stiffly.

I went through to my own room and helped myself to a drink of water from the cooler. The atmosphere was pretty thick. All the water did was help me sweat some more. Then I thought of Miss Digby and grinned. I got her on a soft spot when I said 'Can you find him?' It suggested she might not be able to do it, and that would be all she'd need to turn the town upside down for Thompson. I knew the phone on her desk would be red-hot before she'd give up.

Sam Thompson is one of the best leg-men in the business. He can find out anything about anybody, stay on someone's tail twenty-four hours at a stretch. If he has to. Only if he has to. For Sam suffers from a certain disability. He dislikes all forms of activity, with especial reference to work. To accommodate this shortcoming he has reduced the art of living on a shoestring to fine dimensions. The only time Sam can be coaxed into action is when the pangs of hunger are getting to be more than he can stand. That ought to be about now by my reckoning. His last job for me had been over two weeks before and as far as I knew he hadn't worked since.

I helped myself to an Old Favourite and had it half-smoked when Miss Digby came in.

'I've located Sam,' she announced. 'He will be here within ten minutes. I had to promise him that if he didn't like the job you have for him, he'd get ten dollars any way for his trouble.'

'Good girl,' I told her. Then I remembered and dived in my pocket. 'Find a safe place for this will you?'

She looked at the handwritten agreement from A.I.C.T., lips going prim as she finished reading.

'You seem to be working on something, Mr. Preston. Naturally I don't expect to be taken into your confidence over anything so delicate. May I take it that you are not free to consider anything which may come along?'

'Florence, I can't have you feeling this way. There is a dastardly plot, led by a leading international agent, to steal a toothpaste

34

commercial right off the screen. My appointed task is to prevent it.'

She nodded.

'If it's the ad. I'm thinking of I'll pay you one twenty-five a day to let him get away with it.'

A joke yet. And from Florence that was a rarity to be cherished. Slightly flushed, but clearly pleased with herself, she went out to find some safe place for the agreement.

Sam Thompson made it in eight minutes. His craggy face looked suspiciously round the door, then he shuffled the rest of his short tubby body into the room. The pouched eyes were wary as he sank heavily into a chair.

'Lo, Preston. Flo said to get round here. In a hurry.'

To the best of my knowledge no other living person would dare call Miss Digby Flo.

'No real hurry, Sam. Perhaps Miss Digby was a little over-anxious. Tomorrow would have been fine—' I began, but the balding head was shaking firmly.

'Preston, Preston,' he said sadly, 'Not a spiel. Not to me. You've got me here in a hurry, now you're trying to soft-pedal on the price. It isn't like you, Preston. It hurts me in here.'

The last part would have been more touching if he'd been holding his heart, but Sam was patting his wallet-pocket. I held up my hands.

'All right, I need you tonight. We're in the television business. You know anybody?'

'Anybody? I know everybody. Listen, I'm a personal friend of Huckleberry Hound.'

'Great. Maybe he'll know something. You know the Double Dee Jay Show, the big A.I.C.T. feature Saturday nights?'

'I know of it,' he nodded. 'Personally I can't stand the D-J himself.'

'I won't tell him you said that. That's my client, Donny Jingle. Somebody else besides you doesn't like him. I'm supposed to find out who it is.'

I thought for a moment Thompson had conked off. The heavy-lidded eyes were closed and his chin rested on his chest.

'What do I have to do?' he muttered sleepily.

'Get around a few places. Talk to people. Find out what you can about Jingle.'

He opened one eye and looked at me curiously.

'Any newspaper office could give you a file on the guy a foot thick.'

'No good. It would all be extracts from network news releases, stuff like that. Stuff for public consumption. I want something a little closer to the truth. Can it be done?'

'I guess. May cost a little. Those tee-vee guys, they hang around some expensive bars.'

I looked at the office clock.

36

'It's five forty-five, Sam. I'll see you at Rugolo's Spaghetti at ten forty-five. That's five hours, on the nose. You have what I want and you get fifty. That's ten dollars an hour, brother. I should earn money like that.'

He was up out of the chair.

'You are beginning to get me. This must be a hot potato if you're going to pay that kind of money in a hurry. Anything else?'

'No, I don't think so. See you later.'

After he'd gone, Florence Digby buzzed me. I flicked down the key.

'It's late, Mr. Preston. You want me to lock up?'

'Sure, go ahead. I'm leaving anyway.'

*   *   *

There wasn't time to get myself cleaned up to what I would consider Nicola Hardin standards. I went straight to Raoul's, and perched on a tall, brown leather bar-stool at precisely one minute to six. The bartender was a new man, or maybe I ought to say he was new to me. Raoul's is not a place that normally attracts me very much. I probably hadn't been inside the place in two months. Business was brisk, a lot of home-going business guys sucking up some quick nourishment before heading out into the split-level country. There were one or two women sprinkled about, but nothing special. Certainly nothing to compare

37

with the girl I was waiting for.

I toyed with a large Scotch, clinking the ice-cubes from side to side, wondering what I was doing there. Had I made a date with Nicola for purely personal reasons? On second thoughts delete purely. Or was I hoping to find out something that might give me a lead to whoever wanted Jingle dead? I stared moodily into the glass trying to decide.

'They're usually watching the door expectantly,' murmured a soft voice.

I swung round. Nicola was standing beside me smiling slightly.

'Oh, hallo. Say, I'm sorry, I was thinking about something. Well, it doesn't matter now. Can I get you a drink?'

'I could certainly do with one. What is that, Scotch?'

'It is. And it's the best,' I told her.

'Get me one please. Make it a large one.'

I gathered the drinks and elbowed a pathway between the jostling bar-crowd. There was a small table at the end of the room which was free. Nicola sat down. She was still wearing the blouse I'd noticed in the office, and a black pencil-slim skirt hugged her lower half. She sampled the drink, approved, took a longer pull. Then she smiled and closed her eyes.

'Excellent. I needed that. Donny's just been having one of his tantrums.'

'Oh? Is he prone to them?' I asked.

'Not so much prone,' she corrected. 'He stands right up and welcomes them in. Sometimes I think he positively enjoys them. Anyway you'll see him in action soon enough. You're starting work tomorrow aren't you?'

'I am. Ten a.m. And by the way, thanks for witnessing the man's signature for me.'

She looked at me, slightly puzzled.

'Yes, I was going to ask you about that. Dave said if Donny signed you had insisted on me as a witness. It seemed odd. The only explanation I could think of was that you were trying to impress me as a hundred dollars a day man. Somehow that didn't fit in with what I'd seen of you.'

I grinned.

'Thanks, and you're right. That wasn't the reason. It's really much more simple. Chisum and the other guy—er Shoeman—were the only ones I'd spoken to apart from you. Either one of 'em would swear I made Jingle sign that with a knife at his throat, if he told them to.'

A tiny smile played at the corners of her mouth.

'What makes you think I wouldn't do the same?'

'I don't know,' I confessed. 'You don't strike me as a gal who takes very kindly to being told what to do.'

'Very flattering,' she murmured.

'Not mere flattery, lady,' I reminded her.

'I'm risking a hundred bucks a day on my assessment of you.' She emptied her glass.

'Well, while you're getting it I might as well enjoy it. More, please.'

I went over to the bar and collected two more of the same. When I was back sitting opposite Nicola, she said:

'Why'd you ask me out?'

'Did you ever meet a man who didn't?' I countered.

'One or two. You haven't answered me.'

I thought for a moment before replying. She was a most disconcerting woman, this Nicola Hardin, with a direct way of speaking which made me want to be honest with her.

'I was wondering why when I was waiting for you just now. This business of mine, it's so mixed up with people always, I sometimes have difficulty in understanding my own motives. With you it's like that. When I look at you, there's no problem. I asked you out because you're beautiful and I want to be with you and see if we don't make that thing together. Then when I remember who you are, I wonder whether I'm not trying to get close to you so I can find out what really goes on at Double Dee Jay. Certainly there can't be anybody in a better position than you to answer that one.'

She listened carefully, nodding when I was through.

'That's an honest answer, Mark. More

honest even than I'd expected. I'll return the compliment. I'll tell you why I accepted.'

She toyed with the frosted glass in her hand, sipped at the amber liquid. I sat smoking quietly, not wanting to interrupt at that moment.

'I've been at A.I.C.T. too long. We work hard over there. Not that I'm afraid of work, but our particular work occupies most of the waking day. It has a big drawback. It means that the only people I ever get to meet are television people. I like them. They're a good crowd, mostly. But with them it's the job the whole time. They eat, drink and sleep television. For relaxation they talk about their radio work. It's been months since I had any real opportunity to meet anybody who wasn't in the business. Oh they're a fascinating lot. Talented, enthusiastic and so forth. But when a man's looking at me, the way you are this minute—'

She smiled warmly and I smiled back.

'—I like to be confident he's thinking about me. Not whether it would be a smash idea to do the whole show under green floods. Only last week I was out with someone, and we'd been sitting in his car at the sea without speaking for about five minutes. The moon was doing its best and the water was beautiful. The man turned to me and I thought, 'Now he's going to kiss me, and I'll probably like it.' You know what he said?'

41

'Uh, uh.'

'He said, 'Honey, did Donny happen to mention what the old man said at the programme conference this morning?'

I chuckled.

'The guy had a will of iron. I think I could guarantee not to have a tenth of his will power.'

'So that's why I came. There, I did tell you I'd be honest.'

'I appreciate it. Only trouble is, I'll be in the middle of it all myself tomorrow. Won't that make me one of them?'

'Not for a while, anyway. By the way, that was quite a neat little agreement you made Donny sign. But Donny has one or two neat tricks of his own. Your three days' notice started today. It's in the mail to you now.'

I didn't have to pretend to look bewildered. I meant it.

'Why would he do that? If he doesn't want me on the job all he had to do was refuse to sign at all.'

She nodded.

'It isn't that. Donny reasoned that if you suddenly found out who's doing all this, and then had to have three days' notice, you would be collecting three hundred dollars for doing nothing after the job was finished. So he'll send a notice every day. That way you'll really be on one day's notice any time after the first three days are up.'

I frowned, hoping it looked good-natured.

'Then he has me. Unless I solve it tonight. That way I'll have him.'

She chuckled, that quiet rich sound that started somewhere deep in the green blouse.

'Not really. You can't win. If you find out who it is, and I'm sure you will though perhaps not tonight, you're probably saving Donny's life. So he wins that one too.'

She had me there too.

'O.K.,' I said resignedly. 'Anyway I'm not complaining at those prices. Who do you think it is, Nicola?'

She looked at me sharply over the table.

'You slipped that one in rather smoothly. Well you're bound to ask me sooner or later, so we may as well get it over. I don't know. I've thought and thought and I'm still no nearer. I'd help you if I could, will you believe me?'

'You tell me, and I'll believe you. This or any other subject.'

I meant it.

Her eyes were grateful.

'First I think it's this one, then that. The trouble is I'm too close to it all. If I told you every thought I'd had since this all started it wouldn't do any good, believe me. You'd get a lot of second-hand impressions that may not be of any value at all and I think you'd be better off to come into it new and form your own opinions.'

It was after six-thirty now, and the crowd

was beginning to thin.

'All right,' I agreed. 'Let's not talk about it any more. How about dinner?'

She looked at the tiny watch which was held on the slim wrist by a platinum strap.

'I'm afraid not, Mark. I have to get back.'

'To A.I.C.T.? What time do you get through?'

She patted my hand.

'When they don't need me any more for the day. Maybe eight or even nine.'

We got up and walked slowly to the entrance.

'Don't look so gloomy,' she chided. 'I warned you I wouldn't be carried away by one drink.'

'Two,' I corrected.

'Or even two. Tell you what, call me at eight o'clock and I'll tell you when to come and collect me.'

She squeezed my arm and smiled up at me. I knew this girl was beginning to get to me hard, and wished I knew just how far she meant it.

'I'll call,' I promised.

She wouldn't let me drive her back to the office. Said the walk would do her good. Watching her walk certainly did me good. Two men passing by saw her, and one nudged the other and said something. They both guffawed. I was halfway towards them working up a temper before I realised what I was doing. Then I stopped. What was getting into me, anyhow?

CHAPTER FOUR

I killed time until eight o'clock then called Nicola. She told me she probably wouldn't be able to leave much before ten, and I already had an arrangement with Sam Thompson forty-five minutes after that. Reluctantly I agreed it wouldn't be possible to see her until the next morning. So I had a couple of hours and more left on my hands.

I took a ride round to the offices of the *Monkton Bulletin*. Not because it was any more suitable than the rest of the sheets for what I wanted, but simply because it was the only paper in town with a separate entrance for visitors. That way I had a fair chance of not being seen by any of the reporting or editing staff. There are times when my business has its drawbacks, and one of those times is around newspaper offices. Those guys can smell a story from a ways off.

The night clerk looked up from a twenty-five cent novel. If the contents matched up to the lurid picture on the outside, it seemed to be something I should read.

'Yes, sir?'

'Like to root around in the morgue.' I told

45

him, 'I'm with A.I.C.T., you know, and I'm assigned to the Double Dee Jay show. Like to see the kind of spread the show's been picking up hereabouts. Like maybe catch a few wrinkles, you know.'

'Certainly.' He was interested. As he handed me the blank to fill out he said, 'You mean we have stuff on our files here that your publicity boys haven't got?'

And that almost had me. I laughed, while I was thinking.

'Say, I don't know how familiar you are with these guys, but I sometimes feel they're a little careless about keeping notes of criticisms. I've seen all the praise, the blow-ups and such. What I want is more than that. There must have been times when we put on a turkey, or somebody on the show got a bad press. There's no trace of anything like that on the official files. Guess we're all human, huh?'

I winked at him knowingly. He grinned.

'Guess that's right. There's a one-dollar fee, Mr.—er—' he turned the blank to read what I'd written—'Mr. Chisum.'

I'd put Chisum's name because if it ever occurred to anyone to wonder about my visit, they'd lose all interest when they found out who Chisum was. It seemed like a good idea. It was a rotten idea.

The clerk tucked my dollar bill away in a drawer and led me down a passage to where all the old clippings were filed. He showed me

46

the section I needed and I got on with it. There was certainly plenty to read. There was one file on the programme itself, and separate folders on each of the people chiefly connected with it. Donny Jingle's folder was as thick as the other half dozen put together. There was no folder on Nicola Hardin.

I waded laboriously through. Most of it was plug-material and I didn't waste any time on that. There was one item six months back that was worth a note. It was a newsflash announcing the departure from the show of Whitney Blane the vocalist. She'd been with the show over a year, it said, and felt it was really time she quit. She wanted to widen her activities, make a movie, and there was a Broadway offer she was thinking over. They'd given her a nice big picture, head and shoulders, and she was a girl who deserved a nice big picture. I studied the face so I'd remember it, the shoulders because I enjoyed it.

At the end of an hour I was beginning to get the feel of the show, even some contact with the people. The main file ended abruptly. The *Bulletin* probably hadn't thought it worth while keeping the first handouts on the new programme. There was nothing back in those days to say it would become a national favourite. It could easily have died in a few weeks like so many.

I turned my attention to the individual

47

folders. With these I started at the back and worked forwards in time. One thing struck me right away in Chisum's folder. The first cutting was a brief note saying he and Jingle had arrived at A.I.C.T. from some jungle network. They were going to put on this new show and so forth. But Chisum was described as Jingle's personal manager. It could be a mistake, they are made sometimes. Still, it was curious. There were not many pictures of Chisum, and in them all he was making background for the disc-jockey.

Next I tried the Jingle file. Here I drew blank. If there was a single item in the file to tell me something about the man himself, I couldn't find it. Everything was connected with the family entertainer image. Jingle sparring at a boys' club boxing tournament, Jingle playing Santa Claus at a home for coloured children, Jingle appearing for war charities at no fee. Stuff like that. Not a word about the man behind Jingle. No romances, no gossip, Jingle might be a puppet that A.I.C.T. put back in the trunk every Saturday night after the show. If the file contained a fair run down on his life the poor guy would be better off in the trunk. At least in there no one would want to take his picture.

Of the other files I could make little. Nothing that would give me any reason to suppose any of those people could want Jingle dead. Still I noted a few things, just in case.

The lighting in the *Bulletin* morgue had seemed bright enough when I started, but at the end of a couple of hours I found myself beginning to squint at the fading clippings. Thankfully I closed the last of the folders, put everything back where it came from, and wandered out into the night.

Rugolo's Spaghetti for the benefit of all listeners, is a spaghetti joint and bar run by an Italian named Rugolo. His name is Enrico but he doesn't like to be reminded of it. He claims no American could possibly be named Enrico. So if you want a smile you call him Henry. If you want a drink on the house you call him Hank.

'Hi, Hank.'

I leaned on the counter and waved a hand to him. He came bustling along the bar, a roly-poly good-natured little guy, wreathed in smiles.

'Itsa you, Preston. I'm gladda see ya. Whassa gonna be?'

I ordered Scotch and plain water. He set it up and held out his hand for the money. Things ain't what they were, I reflected sadly. Too many people had cashed in on the Hank thing.

'How's business, Hank?'

'So and so,' he shrugged. 'Look around.'

I looked around. The place was about one-third full. People don't know what they're missing. Even Italians come to eat the

49

spaghetti at Rugolo's.

'Things are bad all over,' I observed in my original way.

'Sure. An' you know why, doncha?' The black eyes were filled with misery. Rugolo was a very emotional character. 'They all stop home. And whaffor? To make-a the eyes turn fonny, all the time stare-a the little box. Me, I like radio.'

He turned and snapped a switch behind him. A soft sound of music eased out of the speakers. Hank smiled.

'Nice, no? Music. Music a man canna listen at, any time. Whaffor should we sit an stare atta box?'

He went away to serve another customer.

Thompson showed at ten-forty. With a sigh he settled beside me, leaning heavily on the counter.

'Brother, the things I do for you.'

'Have a drink, it'll make you feel better,' I recommended.

Thompson screwed up his face.

'I do not want a drink. It will not make me feel better. It will make me feel worse. Terribly worse. I already had so much to drink I only walked part of the way here. The rest I floated.'

He did look somewhat the worse for wear now I looked at him properly.

'All right let's get a quiet table and talk about it.'

We navigated our way carefully, me trying not to spill what was in my glass, Thompson trying not to spill what was inside Thompson. I picked a spot out of earshot of the nearest couple, who were in any case much too engrossed in each other to take any notice of us.

Sam put his head in his hands, rubbed hard at his cheeks and sat up straight.

'You O.K. ?' I asked.

'Sure. Just don't let me smell that liquor. Shall I get on with it?'

'Start when ready, as they say.'

'You told me to get the buzz on a certain party whom I shall not name for reasons of security. Well, brother, you have a job on your hands.'

Maybe it was me who'd had too much to drink, but I couldn't follow that at all.

'Say again?' I queried.

Thompson nodded solemnly.

'Sure. This party we're talking about. He's either being blackmailed or somebody's threatening him.'

'What makes you think that?' I countered.

'Oh for the love of Mike, Preston. Hey, that's not bad, huh? We could make it Mark. We could say, "For the love of Mark," Preston.'

'Very funny. What makes you think what you said just now?'

'Why it's obvious.' He didn't say why it was obvious. 'So naturally you want to know who doesn't like him. And that's what I mean when I say you have a job on your hands.'

Evidently I was going to have to be very patient with Sam Thompson. Especially since he had presumably got stoned for my benefit.

'Not quite with you, Sam. You mean everybody loves the man like a brother?'

He frowned, belched loudly and shook his head.

'Do not mean that. I mean everybody, only everybody in the whole wide world, hates his rotten insides. If he dropped dead tomorrow, there'd be a national holiday.'

I gave him a cigarette, which he finally managed to light from an elusive flame.

'Who doesn't like him, Sam?'

'You name 'em, they hate him,' he replied. 'This guy we're talking about, he's the original heel. One man told me tonight there's a research team up at State still working on a suitable word to describe the guy. So far nothing low enough has come up. So you have a problem, Preston. Most guys have one or two people don't like them. All you have to do is find out which one was in the library when the fatal shot was fired. But this guy is unique. With him it's standing room only in the library. So you have a lot of territory to cover.'

I nodded gloomily. Maybe Sam was exaggerating. Maybe it was really only a few people involved and Sam just happened to hear about them all in the same evening.

Maybe.

'Any names, Sam? Anybody hate him more than the rest?'

'Doubt it. This guy really works at being unpopular. You know his business is spinning discs?'

'I had heard that,' I agreed.

'Well, other people's business is selling discs. To do that you have to get to this certain party. You know how many people have an interest in one little disc?'

'I never thought about it,' I admitted.

'Neither did I. Till tonight anyhow. Now I'm an expert. Let me impress you with my knowledge of the subject. First there's the recording artist, you know the vocalist if it's that type of disc. Then there's the bandleader. There's the guy who wrote the music, and maybe a different guy who wrote the words. There's an arranger, too. All these people are only the start. Behind them there's the company who made the recording, there's the music publisher, the song-plugger, the agents who tenpercents off everybody mentioned so far. We are beginning to gather quite a stack of people, would you say?'

'Now that you mention it, we are,' I nodded.

'All of those people hate this man we're interested in. But they are not the whole story. Everybody on his own show hates him. Everybody in the studios hates him. This,' Thompson shook his head sadly, 'This is not a well-loved man.'

'All right,' I said impatiently. 'Now let's get to why.'

He steered the cigarette into his mouth at the second attempt, drew at it deeply and said,

'By the way I spent eighteen dollars in bars tonight. This is on top of the fifty we agreed, yes?'

'Yes, sure, but get on with it will you, Sam?'

'I am getting on with it,' he replied peevishly. 'Now this man we're talking about, he has a very nasty disposition. He's—er, what's the word I want—power-hungry. The guy is power-hungry. You know what his income is from television and radio work? I'll tell you anyway. It's estimated at a quarter million a year. 'S fact. And that estimate is a low one. The real figure could be up close to half a million. So, money he does not need, right?'

'It should be enough for room and board,' I assented.

'But not enough by itself. Not enough for Mr. J—er—this man we're talking about, he has to push people around as well. Everybody has to kick back. If they don't pay the disc doesn't spin. If they don't spin nobody makes a buck. So all these people we've been talking about, they pay. And if the disc is going to be a top seller, going to be in Donny's Dozen, they pay more. On percentage.'

'How do you mean, percentage?'

'Donny comes in on the take. Two and a half per cent here, four per cent there. It adds up, believe me.'

'I can imagine.'

It was a watertight set-up. In these days of fierce competition in the wax business there's frequently not a hair's breadth between the golden disc and the one that winds up as a remelt. The hair's breadth was Donny Jingle.

'That's not the end of the story,' continued Sam. 'We haven't mentioned the dames yet. Donny likes himself as a great lover. The dames don't have to give any money. For them he has a special offer. So the dames especially don't like him too well. The successful ones hate him because of the way they got successful. The others, the ones who think his prices are too high, they hate him because they haven't made the grade. This is a sweet guy, this feller we're talking about.'

'Let me think about it a while, Sam.'

He seemed glad enough of the chance just to sit there trying to keep awake. I sipped at my drink and thought over what he'd been telling me. It wasn't an encouraging picture. It wasn't even impossible that more than one person was involved in trying to clean up the neighbourhood where Donny Jingle lived. Certainly it would mean very little co-operation from people like that, if they thought they might help someone else do their cleaning up for them by withholding information. And I was only one man.

There was a disc programme on the radio while I was deep in thought. With half an ear, I was aware of the smooth soft voice of a girl singer, as she throbbed out some lyric about being all alone in the night. That was me. I reflected, old Hawkshaw Preston, all alone in the night, with nobody even likely to give a hand when they knew who it would help besides me. The voice faded softly down and an announcer gave a time check. It was eleven p.m. he told us and time for our two minute news roundup. President Kennedy had said something. Kruschev had said something different. The union boss had said he'd welcome an investigation of the union's affairs. An airliner was missing somewhere in Central America. Donny Jingle, tee-vee and radio personality—

Donny Jingle. Suddenly I was listening with both ears.

'—died a few minutes ago in a mystery explosion outside the offices of ·the Amalgamated Inter-Coastal Television Company. Donny who—'

I turned out, and stood up.

'Catch up with the rest later, Sam,' I said quickly.

'Hm?'

Thompson opened one eye and stared up at me blearily.

'Got to go. Can you get home all right or

56

shall I call a cab?'

'No need,' he assured me. 'What's the big rush?'

'Jingle. Somebody got to him. He's dead.'

He digested this before replying. Then he said:

'Good.'

As I left he was almost asleep.

CHAPTER FIVE

Ten minutes later I reached the A.I.C.T. building. There was no room for the Chev in front so I went round to the visitors space at the side again. The vestibule was thronged with people. They wore as many different kinds of dress as you could dream up. Tuxedos, lounge suits, bandjackets, leather. There was even one dame with a coat thrown loosely over a swim suit. I never did find out who she was.

Elbowing my way through the excited, chattering crowd, I made it to reception. There were four different girls on duty now, all with raven hair. What a stroke of luck for the network, I reflected. With their black hair, crisp white blouses and black skirts, these four looked to be in half-mourning already. Their faces were solemn, troubled. They were all busy explaining to the mob that pressed against the counter that there was no further news yet, that no interviews were being granted at the moment, that they didn't know about funeral arrangements. And a hundred other things. I finally managed to corner one of them.

'I want to see Chisum or Shoeman. Somebody on the Double Dee Jay.'

She looked at me with sad eyes.

'I'm sorry, it's not possible at present. If you'll leave your telephone number I'll call when—'

'It's possible for me honey. I work here, on the show. Call 'em, tell 'em I'm here. Mark Preston.'

She was doubtful. I said:

'Ask Nicola Hardin. Or better still call up Kingworth if he's here.'

That was the clincher. She went back to her desk, put the pink telephone to her ear and dialled.

'O.K., Mr. Preston. You can go on up.'

'Thanks.'

I pushed a path towards the elevators. Here the operators stood in a solemn, unmoving line staring back at the crowd who were arguing with everyone in sight about their right to go upstairs. In front of the elevator men stood a large man in a rumpled blue suit. He was the law. As I eased to the front of the crowd he held up a hand.

'Sorry, nobody goes up,' he told me.

'I have clearance,' I replied. 'Name of Preston.'

He turned to the uniformed brigade behind him.

'Mr. Preston wants to go up,' he said. 'Mean anything.'

They all shook their heads.

'Never seen him before,' said one.

Then the man next to him spoke.

'Wait a minute, Peggy's waving.'

We all turned to see who Peggy was. She turned out to be the sorrowful girl who'd been talking to me.

'O.K. for up, she says,' my favourite elevator man told the cop.

'Well, I guess it's all right,' he rumbled reluctantly. 'If she says so, you can bet on it, officer.'

So I went up. As the doors of the elevator slid smoothly across I could not resist a feeling of smugness at the curious and hostile expressions of the crowd who waited impatiently below.

At twelve the big ugly character, Charlie, was waiting as I emerged.

'Hi, Charlie,' I greeted.

'Sorry,' he grunted. 'I got orders. No talking to anybody.'

We trooped along to Double Dee Jay in silence. Charlie unlocked the door to the programme offices, and after we were in, solemnly locked it again. Then he led me through to Nicola Hardin's room. It was empty. Charlie nodded towards Jingle's office.

'In there.'

I waited for him to lead the way but he turned around and went out. I knocked on Jingle's door and went in.

They were sitting around on any available surface. Shoeman, Nicola, a tall slim man whom I recognised as Chrazy Chris, the bandleader on the Double Dee Jay, three men I'd never seen before.

And Donny Jingle.

I stared at him. The others watched me curiously, or dispassionately in some cases. I'd get round to them in a moment. Right now I couldn't take my eyes off Jingle.

'You'll be Mr. Preston?'

One of the men who was new to me barked out the words. Reluctantly I looked away from the trembling and sweating disc jockey and towards the speaker. He was below average height, a fat man with grey bushy hair either side of a shining bald scalp. His face was not the jolly face you expect on a man of his proportions. There was petulance there, and the signs of temper.

'I'm Preston,' I acknowledged.

'I am Vance Kingworth, vice-president of this network, Mr. Preston. You have arrived at an opportune moment. Please find a seat and we'll get on with the proceedings.'

That was when I finally registered

something that would have arrived sooner, if the shock of seeing Jingle hadn't driven it out of my mind.

'Where's Dave Chisum?' I asked.

Several people shifted uncomfortably. Jingle sighed and put his hands to his face.

'It was Dave who died tonight,' explained Kingworth. 'He got into Donny's automobile and it blew up. People knew the car, and naturally assumed it was Donny. The news got to a couple of radio stations outside this network and was released before we had a chance to make an official statement. They were so anxious to scoop A.I.C.T. they forgot the basic rule that information given to the public must be accurate.'

It was evident from Kingworth's tone, that even under these circumstances it was a pleasure to see the rival stations embarrassed. I was more concerned about Chisum. Poor, anxious, tubby Dave. The man who wanted to keep afloat in a pond where the other fish were mostly barracuda. The guy who would not willingly give up his two hundred and fifty bucks a week. The one who was now being pieced back together in some police laboratory, so there would be something recognisable for his family to identify.

Jingle seemed to be taking it hard, but I couldn't judge the reason. It could be because a friend had been blown to pieces, or on the other hand it could simply be that he was thinking it might have been him in the car. And that when the killer found out he'd goofed, he'd try again.

It was hard to guess what anyone else in the room was feeling, if anything. Mostly they seemed to be just sitting there, waiting for the great Kingworth to give them a lead on how they felt. Then they would all be sad, exultant, relieved or any other emotion the great man selected. I tried to catch Nicola's eye, but she avoided my glance. Kingworth coughed. He was waiting for me to join the class. I found a wooden chair against the wall by the door and parked.

'Now,' barked Kingworth, 'To business. That is, if you're feeling quite up to it, Donny.'

The bark was noticeably more of a purr when he addressed his top performer. Jingle nodded wearily.

'Sure, V.K., I'm all right. Might as well get to it.'

Kingworth nodded, satisfied. A ritual had been observed. The great business man had shown proper respect for the finer feelings, and the subject had bravely acknowledged that business must come first.

'All of us in this room know that Donny has been threatened lately, and that there have previously been two unsuccessful attempts on his life. This time the madman did get a victim, but the wrong man. Poor Dave is dead out there instead of Donny. I have told the police department that I would hold a meeting in this office at eleven thirty, at which I would arrange for the people in this organisation most closely connected with Dave to be present. That gives us precisely fourteen minutes in which to make several decisions of importance.'

He glared all round the room as if expecting a heckler. There was nobody present who would dare to take on the job. I didn't count, I was an outsider.

'The point is this,' resumed the fat man. 'No publicity has ever been given to the previous attacks on Donny. To my knowledge only those present are aware that they took place. Anybody add anything to that, before I continue?'

Nobody stirred.

'Very well. Now we can't run a show like Double Dee Jay if we are to have a lot of police officers parading around the offices and the studios trying to find out who's after Donny. A show generates an atmosphere of its own, particularly a family show like Double Dee Jay. The atmosphere is transmitted to Joe Public, and what kind of an atmosphere is that going to be if there's some tough policeman sitting beside every camera, watching every expression? An alternative is open to us.'

Having painted a black picture for the audience, he now notched up his voice a couple of places as we approached the great solution. He almost beamed.

'Poor Dave Chisum is the man who died. He's the one the police are interested in. He's the man whose picture will be in every tabloid tomorrow morning. Who would want to kill Dave? Nobody, so far as we know. Certainly nobody around here even disliked him. If we let the police proceed on the assumption that Dave Chisum was the intended victim, they'll spend very little time holding up our affairs. Just hang on a while, Chris.'

The bandleader had been about to chip in, but Kingworth clipped him off before he got started.

'I know there'll be questions, some discussion. But first, hear me through. Naturally I do not suggest we let it go at that. We bring in one of the big private firms whose business it is to handle this sort of thing—no offence to you, Preston, but this will not be a one-man operation, and we tell these people the real story, let them proceed with an investigation based on the true facts. That way we'll keep it the way we want it. In the family and behind the scenes. Now before I throw the discussion open let me say I've already mentioned this to Donny. He's the one most concerned, the target for this killer, and it could be his life we're talking about. He wasn't keen at first, but I think he now sees it's the best thing for Double Dee Jay and the network. And this has to be our prime consideration. All right. Questions.'

Chrazy Chris spoke first.

'I don't want to talk out of turn, Mr. Kingworth, and you'll correct me if I'm wrong. But aren't we going a little fast here? Seems to me we'd be better occupied mourning Dave Chisum, and working out what we're gonna do to help his wife and kids.'

That was the first sensible thing I'd heard so far, and even with my limited knowledge of A.I.C.T., I had some measure of the guts it took to say it. I looked at the musician with respect. The look he got from Kingworth was a compound of many things, respect not being one of them.

'Why naturally, Chris, of course. I hope I'm not getting the wrong atmosphere into this little talk. It's just I took it for granted we all knew the way we felt about Dave. Maybe I was wrong, but I assumed we didn't need to hold a public wailing to show how deep this thing about Dave Chisum goes. I can only plead that everything's happened so fast, maybe I did get things in the wrong sequence. I want to thank you for putting me back on the rails, Chris. Of course, I have already taken it on my own authority to say that Dave Chisum will get the treatment.'

There were murmurs of approval from several quarters. The boss had evidently said the right thing, even though I didn't know what he was talking about. I made a mental note to find out just what he meant by 'the treatment.'

'Mr. Kingworth, sir,' Mr. Shoeman was evidently surprised at his own temerity in speaking. 'The car. How do we explain the car? If the guy who put the bomb in there meant it for Dave he was taking a long chance wasn't he?'

Good point. One or two nodded agreement, Kingworth included. Shoeman's relief at not having talked out of turn was comical.

'You're absolutely right, Mo, of course,' assented the big boss. 'Fortunately we shall be able to say Donny has not been feeling too well lately, at the end of a long working day. He has not felt sufficiently well to take charge of an automobile, the way the roads are these nights. So he has fallen into the habit of lending that car to Dave each evening. He has been doing this for several nights past to my knowledge, and probably others know about it. We can produce the staff driver who has had the job of driving Donny home on those nights. So it probably would not be too difficult for anyone who was interested enough to find out.'

Shoeman nodded as though completely satisfied. The nod, I felt sure, would have been the same if Kingworth had told him to go and jump out of a window.

One of the two men, whom I still hadn't identified but who turned out to be script-writers for the show, said:

'About this atmosphere thing, sir. Things have been getting a little out of hand around here as it is. Several people are convinced all this is being done by somebody we all know. I take your point about the police making us all feel as if we were in San Quentin, but I'm not certain we aren't going to find something almost as bad springing up in any case. After all, if there's any reason to suppose one of us killed Dave Chisum it isn't going to do much for the happy family bit, is it?'

Kingworth's voice was like a whiplash.

'I want to hear no more of that kind of talk from anybody. The whole idea is ridiculous. But it does bring me to something I meant to say earlier. When the investigators from the private company go to work, you must all be prepared to co-operate with them every inch of the way. In order to eliminate yourselves from further enquiries you will authorise them one hundred per cent to vet your bank accounts, go into your homes, talk to your friends. This, I do not ask. I am simply making an announcement.'

He glared all round the room again, his eyes scorching briefly at each person in turn. One or two shifted in their seats, but again nobody contradicted him.

'It is now eleven twenty-eight. The police will be here in two minutes. I take it, if there are no further questions, that we have reached agreement on the line we shall take.'

67

There were no further questions. There was, regrettably, one interruption. From me.

'You're forgetting something, Mr. Kingworth. Me.'

'You?' He frowned slightly, as though not getting the point. 'You are an employee here, Preston. For all practical purposes you are also a stranger. You will of course, do as you are told. And now that I am reminded of your presence, please leave before the police get here. None of this is anything to do with you. There will be a cheque in the mail tomorrow, for one month's advance salary, at the inflated value you put on your services. I think that is quite generous. You are now free to leave.'

He turned his face away from me, as though to deal with the next minor matter which required his attention. The conceit of the man was overpowering.

'I'm staying,' I told him. 'And since the police will arrive at any second, I advise you to listen to what I'm going to say, Kingworth.'

I dropped the 'Mr.' deliberately and was rewarded by the gaping faces of some of those present. In particular, I had difficulty in not laughing at Mo Shoeman's worried look, which grew about six extra wrinkles as I spoke.

'I am a licensed private investigator. A licence is something which can be revoked. It is my duty under the terms of that licence to keep the police fully informed of any developments in a felony case. I never try to outsmart the police. It doesn't pay. You think you can do it by holding this phoney board meeting here, but you're wrong. What you're trying to do wouldn't fool the police for long, even without me. And you, let me emphasise, are not without me.'

'This is terrible,' Kingworth didn't waste time on anger. His watch advised him against that. 'Are you telling me you are deliberately about to jeopardise the livelihood of everyone in this room?'

'No,' I shook my head. 'I'm telling you I'm going to start off right with the law over this. And, incidentally, give friend Jingle here a slightly better chance of survival.'

The look Jingle gave me could have been gratitude if he'd been certain the boss wasn't looking. The telephone by Kingworth's hand pinged. He picked it up and listened. 'Very well,' he said. Then he put the phone down. 'The police are on their way up. We haven't much time.'

'Time for me to say one more thing. In law, conspiracy is a crime. What you've tried to do here the last fifteen minutes was to concoct a conspiracy. I'll go this far. I won't report it. Nobody would gain anything, and you would personally finish up in jail. When the police get here tell them nothing but the plain unvarnished truth.'

I stared him straight in the face while I spoke. In his sixty odd years I'd bet Vance

Kingworth never hated anybody the way he hated me at that moment. The others watched him, ready to jump in whichever direction he indicated. His voice was like dry ice.

'Very well, you all heard this gentleman. Do as he says.'

CHAPTER SIX

The Police Department was represented by three men. First through the door was a man in a tuxedo with a light topcoat. He was Wayne Durrant the assistant commissioner. I happened to know he seldom made personal visits on homicide calls. Just showed what assessment the community places on its Saturday night entertainment. Behind him came John Rourke and Gil Randall, lieutenant and sergeant respectively of the Homicide detail. Randall spotted me at once and spoke softly to Rourke, who turned his head, saw me and looked away. Durrant walked up to Kingworth's desk.

'I am Wayne Durrant, Assistant Commissioner of police, sir.'

He held out his hand and Kingworth touched it briefly. I thought I detected a slight shadow cross his face at the word 'Assistant'. Durrant must have spotted it too.

'I know the Commissioner would wish me to

extend his apologies for not being able to attend personally, sir. He is at a convention in Washington at present.'

Kingworth acknowledged this with a slight smile. After all, the head man could hardly have come back from Washington in forty minutes. And this assistant person evidently knew who it was he was talking to. He decided to make the best of it.

'Mr. Durrant,' he bowed his head slightly. 'Perhaps we should have a preliminary chat in my private suite.'

'Very good of you to suggest it, sir. In the meantime, perhaps you would not object if my officers were to proceed with their enquiries with these good people here?'

Kingworth hesitated only fractionally. I knew he was looking at me from behind those pouches over his eyes. I grinned at him blandly.

'Certainly not, no objection whatever. We've no secrets here, Mr. Commissioner.'

Turning to Rourke and Randall he said:

'Please continue, and feel free to use any of the office services which may help.'

Rourke acknowledged this little speech, and Kingworth and Durrant left the room. There was a noticeable relaxing of the atmosphere when the vice president of the network was gone. The change of mood was not lost on Rourke. Nothing ever is.

'Well, folks, I want to tell you we appreciate

your coming here like this. We'll get through as quickly as we can, but I'll have to ask you to be patient, and remember this is a homicide matter. Bound to take up a little time.'

While he was talking he looked at each person in turn. I don't know what Rourke does with those looks of his, but he has almost thirty years of enviable reputation behind him, and I know the looks fit in the pattern somewhere.

'Here's a familiar face, lieutenant,' Randall reminded him. 'Should we start with Mr. Preston?'

The others looked at the man who'd drawn the short straw. I got up.

'Why not? You going to do it in here?'

'No,' Rourke decided. 'Is there a smaller room we could use?'

'There's Chisum's own office.'

I led them out, and conversation buzzed quickly as the door closed behind us. In Chisum's room Rourke settled wearily behind the desk. Randall remained standing, and I parked in the same plastic chair I'd used before.

'You're getting better, Mark,' observed Rourke. 'Now you're turning up at the scene of the crime before it's committed. How come?'

'No catch,' I replied.

He heaved his shoulders.

'It's easy. We fixed for Kingworth to have everybody here who's important on the programme. When we get here we find you.

You're not going to tell me Kingworth hired you since this thing happened, are you?'

'Oh, I see. No, I'm not going to tell you that. I was hired today.'

'To do what?'

'Find out who's been threatening Donny Jingle.'

'Ah hah.'

Rourke and Randall exchanged quick glances. Rourke then fished in his pockets and found one of his obnoxious little Spanish cigars.

'Better sit down. Gil,' he advised. 'I have a feeling we're going to have a profitable conversation with this guy for once.'

'Always co-operate with the department, John. You know that,' I told him.

'I know nothing of the kind,' he replied evenly. 'I know you're always under my feet when anything blows up around this town. I know you have an apartment over at Parkside the Commissioner himself couldn't afford. Considering your limited ability, I sometimes wonder just why you should earn, all by yourself, about the same annual income as the entire Robbery detail of the Monkton City P.D. And that is one of our largest details. You mean to tell me you do all that just by co-operating with an old flatfoot like me?'

'That's part of it anyway.'

'O.K. Soo-operate. Tell me something about this tee-vee circus here. I'm especially interested in that last part about this Donny Jingle.'

I started to talk. There were few questions as I went along. Rourke contented himself by sitting with his head tilted back in the chair, poisoning the atmosphere with clouds of pungent yellow smoke. Gill Randall was now sitting at the side of the desk. Nobody made any notes. With these two, notes were unnecessary.

'So this guy we have on the slab has no business to be dead, you say?' queried Rourke.

'I didn't say that,' I corrected. 'What I am saying is there have been previous attempts to kill Donny Jingle. There may not be any connection at all. There could be someone else, someone who meant to kill Dave Chisum and did.'

'Which would leave us with two killers to locate,' grumbled Randall. 'One apprentice and one full-fledged. What do you say, lieutenant?'

Rourke tilted his head far enough to look at me while he answered the sergeant.

'I say no. I say Preston has the right attitude. He keeps an open mind. Doesn't pre-judge the issue. Very good, very good. That's week six at police training school, isn't it, Gil?'

'Week four,' Randall contradicted. 'Since your time they speeded things up some.'

He grinned widely at his chief. They were as thick as thieves, these two. Rourke glared back.

'At the expense of thoroughness, sergeant. Now, as I say, I approve of your attitude, Preston, but I don't buy. A television programme like this Double Dee Jay is a kind of closed circuit as far as people are concerned. Kind of like a family, happy or otherwise. I can't afford an open mind like you. With me, two killers out of one group of people is too many. I'll probably have enough trouble finding just one. I say there's a connection. What else can you tell me?'

I thought about what I had said so far. All I'd given the police officers was fact. There was nothing in the rule book said I had to part with any theory. So I'd not mentioned Sam Thompson, and his bag of rumours. That was a little extra I would need up my sleeve if I was going to compete with these professionals. And I was going to compete. Although I hadn't a client, strictly speaking, I was still on the payroll of A.I.C.T. or the Donny Jingle set-up, and at a hundred bucks a day I felt they ought to get some kind of service.

'I've given you all the facts, John,' I told him.

'Sure. How about some side information. Like, for example what do you make of this bunch here?'

'I wasn't hired till late this afternoon. Haven't had much chance to do anything yet. As I already told you, I was supposed to report

75

tomorrow morning.'

'H'm. Then what're you doing here now?'

'I heard the newscast at eleven. According to that, Jingle was dead. Seeing I'd been hired to prevent that, it seemed to me I better get down here and find out what happened.'

'Uh huh. And now you know?'

'Not really. Kingworth didn't tell me much.'

'Well, sergeant, since this private person has told us what he knows, I think we might tell him the facts. Just the ones he could read in his newspaper tomorrow, naturally.'

Gil Randall nodded and began to recite.

'At ten forty eight this evening, David Chisum, assistant to one Donny Jingle, television performer, left this building by a side entrance normally reserved for the use of the senior executives of the company. Chisum was not one of those people. He was seen leaving by Washington Lincoln Moses, employed here as a janitor. The janitor thought at first it was Jingle, because he recognised the coat Chisum was wearing. The victim walked across to the reserved parking space and unlocked Jingle's car. Then he climbed in and pressed the starter. A connection had been made between the starter button and a home-made bomb under the dash. The bomb exploded, Chisum received multiple injuries and died a few seconds later. Officer Rogan was on foot patrol duty close by. He heard the explosion and arrived within one minute. A lot of people had gathered round by then. Some of these were employees of the company. They told Rogan the dead man was Jingle. The light out in the lot isn't good, and many of Chisum's injuries were facial. However there's no doubt the witnesses were really identifying the automobile and the overcoat, both of which were Jingle's property.'

He stopped, looked at Rourke.

'Thanks, Gil. That's the first real information I've had on what happened,' I told him.

He nodded in acknowledgement. Rourke said:

'That's a nice-looking girl, that dark one in there. Did I say something wrong?'

That's what I mean about Rourke. He kind of edges these things in sidewise. Too quickly for me to restrain whatever he saw in my face at the mention of Nicola.

'Nothing at all,' I assured him. 'Yes, she's a good-looker.'

'Do 'emselves pretty well, I fancy, these tee vee guys. All these actresses and singers and all. Would she be somebody's very private secretary, John?'

'She works for Jingle, if that's what you mean.'

I tried to sound natural and relaxed. It wasn't easy when I was trying to keep down my rising temper, suspecting what would come next.

'I heard about this Jingle, lieutenant,' contributed Randall. 'He goes for the girls. All kinds.'

'Zasso?' Rourke sounded interested. 'What kind of a private secretary do you figure this one, John? Just desk work, maybe?'

Randall snorted with derision. I said tightly:

'I imagine so.'

The grizzled detective carried on as if I hadn't spoken.

'Then again if she's just for work, what's she doing here this hour of the night? Most of the offices I know are all through, have been for hours.'

'She's here late quite a lot,' I informed him. 'Jingle likes to clear as much as he can before he quits at night.'

'Uh huh.'

He tilted his head back again and puffed contentedly at the small cigar. I noted with relief it was over half-smoked.

'And when Jingle took you on for this desperate assignment,' Rourke couldn't keep the amusement out of his voice. Couldn't or wouldn't. 'When he hired you this afternoon, he made a point of telling you what time the girl got off duty? Your reputation must be getting around.'

'We chanced to be talking. while I waited,' I explained patiently. 'This was just one of those little things that get mentioned in a casual conversation, that's all.'

'And there's nothing you haven't told us?'

'You've had all my facts,' I insisted.

' 'Kay, Mark. Let me tell you just one little thing before you leave this room. You see the way things are here. The guy's not even cold yet, and already we have the assistant commissioner here in person sirring everybody. That's the kind of deal this is, a big pressure—do something about it. I don't want to get tough with you, but just be sure you keep in touch. I want to know every little thing you find out. Everything. Catch?'

'Got it.'

I made for the door.

'Oh and send in your girl-friend,' Rourke called.

Randall chuckled. I bit back whatever it was I'd been going to say, and shut the door. Crossing Nicola's office I looked in at the others.

'Miss Hardin, will you come please.'

She got up and walked over without looking into my face. I took one step back to let her come through, also so the others wouldn't hear what I said.

'I'll wait for you, honey. It won't take long.'

She looked up at me then and I could see the trouble in her eyes.

'No, Mark. Not tonight. Not after all this.'

'Tomorrow?'

She shook her head:

'I don't know. Perhaps.'

Then she went to talk to the police officers. I wished I'd known what was upsetting her. Or maybe I was forgetting there'd been sudden death among these people and it wasn't their stock-in-trade as it was mine. I went back to the others. Jingle said nervously:

'Kept you a helluva time didn't they? What's it all about?'

He sounded irritable and considering he only just failed to qualify for a mortuary I couldn't blame him.

'I don't know what it's all about,' I reminded him.

'That's what I've been doing all this time. Trying to convince the police.'

I went over and sat down next to the bandleader, Chrazy Chris. He was leaning forwards, elbows on knees, smoking moodily. He took no notice of me.

Everybody else was quiet. Even Mo Shoeman seemed finally to have used it all up. Jingle suddenly jumped to his feet.

'I can't stand this,' he grumbled. 'Sitting around here like it was a wake.'

Beside me, the musician raised his head and eyed the disc-jockey balefully.

'But that's what it is, ain't it? Dave Chisum got dead just an hour ago. What do you want, champagne and a sixteen-year-old virgin?'

'That'll be enough outa you. I can get a dozen foot-bangers where you came from and don't you forget it,' replied Jingle nastily.

'Say, Donny—'

One of the script boys got up quickly, sensing trouble and knowing this wasn't the time.

'Well?'

Jingle still didn't take his eyes off Chris.

'I was thinking, since we're here and all, I mean don't think I haven't any respect about Dave or anything, but you're right, we'll go crazy just sitting here. Lou and I have an outline for that charity thing next month. We could maybe just run through it, you know, do a little work, get our minds busy.'

Jingle frowned, and looked thoughtfully at the speaker.

'Well, I take it back. Last week I told you you never had an idea in your whole miserable life. But you made it, you finally came through, boy. What's the outline?'

He crossed to the two men, and together they went to a table at the end of the room. Here Lou took some paper from an inside pocket and spread it out. They all leaned on the table, and began to talk in low, urgent voices.

The bandleader resumed his solitary smoking. Keeping my voice low I said:

'Where do I find Whitney Blane?'

He turned quickly to look at me.

'Why d'you ask?'

'Like to talk to her. Do you know where she

is?'

He studied me carefully before replying.

'I might. But I don't know where you figure in all this.'

'You know as much as anybody else,' I told him. 'I'm going to find out who killed Chisum.'

'Oh sure,' he mocked. 'Why not leave it to the law? I hear they're good at it.'

'You hear right. Only they're outside. I'm inside, at least partly.'

He nodded.

'That's what bothers me. I know this crowd. I ought to, it's my crowd. You know what Kingworth would do if he had his way? He'd get this quietened off somehow. Say Dave killed himself, or bled to death from a shaving cut. Anything to get the heat off his lousy network. What will the sponsors say? Anyhow, I don't know whether I trust you. You could be hired to keep ahead of the police, make sure they don't come up with anything.'

'No I couldn't,' I said evenly. 'You heard me face Vance Kingworth down before the police came.'

Chris dropped his cigarette butt on the deep pile carpet and ground it carefully under his heel. It seemed a long time before he replied.

'I'll take a chance,' he breathed. 'You'll find out anyhow. She's at the Bellevue Apartments. Number 63.'

'Thanks.'

I started to get up, but he put a hand on my

arm. 'You going there now?'

'Yes. Why?'

'Nothing. Look, when I get through with the rackets commission I'll be at a place called Gloomy Sunday. You know where that is?'

I nodded. I'd heard of the place, a meeting-spot for jazz musicians. I'd never been there before.

'I'll be there till about three-thirty,' he told me. 'And one more thing, you're going to see Whitney. Tell her hallo from me, and don't be too quick to judge people.'

I didn't know whether he meant Whitney Blane, singer, or Chrazy Chris, bandleader. On the way out of the room I called out goodnight but nobody answered.

CHAPTER SEVEN

The Bellevue Apartments was one of those quiet luxury deals up on Parkside Heights, not too far from home for me. Number 63 was no different on the outside from any of the other doors I passed while looking for it. The buzzer sounded clearly out in the hall. After a short wait I gave it another push. This time I got results. The door opened a crack and an eye was pushed up close to the thin shaft of light.

'Whitney Blane?' I asked.

The door was opened wide now and I was

looking at five feet five inches of beautifully distributed female. She wore tight red slacks that could have been painted on. Over these, a checked lumberjack shirt did nothing to keep the high pouting breasts any secret. Her throat and neck were like ivory. She had an oval face with strong cheekbones and her eyes were deep blue. Cherry-coloured hair tumbled in disarray around her head but I was not in the mood to criticise. Except perhaps on one count. The lady was not what you'd call stone cold sober.

'You're pretty,' she said solemnly, poking me in the chest with her finger. 'C'mon in, the party's just getting started.'

I followed her inside, and closed the door. The apartment was done out in white-painted furniture, frail and expensive. So the glare wouldn't hurt the eyes, the padding was all red silk. The cushions were red silk too, and the windows were screened by wall-length red velvet curtains with huge gold tassels. It was all like some elaborate gag by a man who'd spent his life designing movie-theatre lobbies. It shrieked.

Whitney Blane walked across to a side table, the tight little bottom rolling provocatively. I had a feeling it wasn't being done for my benefit, and that was its normal method of progress. The party consisted of two brandy bottles, the first of which was already half-empty. If there were any other people I couldn't see them.

'Brandy O.K. ?' she demanded.

'Just a little,' I said. 'I've been drinking scotch.'

'Oh.' She stood and pondered this, frowning in concentration. 'Sorry, no scotch, mister. It'll have to be brandy.'

She splashed herself about four fingers of the stuff. I winced. Brandy is not something to drink like orange juice. Especially brandy with that label. Setting her own glass down with exaggerated care she looked around for another, found it and poured for me.

'That's plenty, thanks,' I stopped her.

Then she brought it across, handed it to me and raised her drink.

'Here's to it, whatever it is.'

I grunted and sipped at the golden liquid. A warm comfortable feeling seeped slowly through me as the drink hit bottom. The vocalist wasn't so delicate, pouring the stuff away as if the important thing was to get the glass empty. I wondered whether she had drunk the whole half of a fifth that evening. Before I could decide that I'd have to know what her normal consumption was, but on the surface I'd be prepared to guess it was on the high side.

'Well, let's sit down.'

She waited till I found a chair that looked as if it wouldn't collapse under me. Once I was seated she came and parked on the arm, one red leg resting against mine.

'There now, we have a party, or soon will. I'm glad you came, pretty man. And before this little wingding is through you're going to be glad too.'

She tilted her head to one side and smiled. Her face was about two feet away, and the animal warmth of the girl was not something I'd be able to ignore indefinitely.

'Miss Blane—' I began.

'Wait, wait. You're ahead of me. I still don't know who you are. Not that it'll change anything, but does any kind of name go with those shoulders?'

'Preston. Mark Preston.'

'Ah.'

Moving gently against me she kissed me softly on the mouth. I didn't grab her, but I didn't ignore the kiss either. That would have taken a better man than me. She moved away again and smiled lazily.

'How do you do, Mr. Mark Preston. That was nice. Gentle and nice. I think we'll have a lovely party, don't you?'

I didn't want to talk about that, or even think about it. It would take very little for me to give my full attention to the party possibilities, and that was not the reason I'd come. I said seriously:

'Aren't you going to ask me who I am, and what I'm doing here?'

'Mr. Preston,' she reproved, 'I have been

around a long time. If I was standing in the snow without anything to eat and a man handed me a steak dinner, you think I'd ask him where he got it?'

The steak dinner sat and thought that one through. She chuckled.

'Here I was having a party all by myself. I have the place and the booze. I hadn't got around to realising there was no man, but it would have come to me later. In spades. Then you walk in. I have a mirror, Mr. Preston. How many men do you suppose would want to worry about the details?'

She had me there. Then she sighed.

'O.K. I can see by the look on your face you want to talk about something. Let's get it over with, but don't take too long. I'm a woman of moods, my friend. You break up the one I'm in and I can't guarantee to bring it back.'

She was prepared to be offended, and I couldn't predict how she'd react if that happened.

'Don't worry about it, beautiful. I can guarantee to bring it back,' I assured her.

'Well now,' she snuggled against me, 'I was beginning to feel like the girl in the commercials.'

'They've got nothing like you in the commercials,' I told her. 'Now, will you listen for a minute?'

'One minute? Sure.'

'You were resident on the Double Dee jay

show a long time.'

She stiffened slightly.

'Sure. Everybody knows that. What about it?'

'I've been wondering why you quit the show.'

Pushing herself away she looked up into my face.

'Who wants to know?' she demanded.

I indicated the drink in my hand.

'Mark Preston, brandy drinker.'

'But you didn't come here as a brandy drinker,' she pointed out. 'You didn't even know there was any brandy till you got inside. You a reporter, come here because of what happened tonight?'

It was too good an excuse to reject.

'Sort of,' I admitted. 'I want to get an unusual angle on the show, so I'm leaving the present performers to the other guys. I'm visiting the people who've been associated with the programme in the past. You know, get a long-distance shot.'

She laughed, a brittle, harsh sound.

'I was right about you. You are smart. But you're going to get a different story to the other guys, brother. You are going to get the truth. And it won't do you a damned bit of good, because you won't be allowed to print a word.'

'I don't think I'm with you.'

She rubbed herself softly against me.

'All in good time, Preston. You will be.'

'That's not what I meant, and you know it,' I protested feebly. But I didn't ask her to stop. 'What won't they let me print?'

'All right,' she said wearily. 'If you have to have it, let's get it over with. Let's make it short and sweet, and get back to the party. Deal?'

She uncurled herself from my chair, went and sank deep in a low-backed affair opposite.

'What do you want—I recall those glittering nights of laughter and champagne?'

'Not exactly. I'd prefer something closer to the facts.'

'I figured. Well now, Mark Preston, stop me if you've seen this picture before. It sounds like an old B movie, sponsored by the handkerchief industry. Do you have a violin?'

'Didn't think to bring it with me,' I apologised.

She sniffed and emptied her glass, waving her free hand for me to wait. I waited.

'You ever heard me sing?' she demanded.

'A few times.'

'I can tell by your voice you didn't like it. No, no don't bother to contradict me. It was getting so I didn't like it either. You got a cigarette?'

I passed out the Old Favourites and she accepted a light.

'I've been a singer—oh—'bout six years now. Started out the usual way, the small town bit, you know. I was beginning to settle down nicely, had a regular half-hour show on the local radio station. Nothing fabulous, but I earned a dollar. Waxed a few, here and there, they didn't win any prizes. But I was rubbing along, you know, no complaints. That's when my brother took a hand.'

'Your brother?' I queried.

'Yeah. He was in the racket, here in Monkton. I did a souped-up version of Blue Moon with a few progressive musicians. It was pretty good, too. Not commercial, but a nice professional piece of modern if you like it. My brother sold it to a famous disc-jockey. Guess who?'

'Jingle.'

'Sure, Jingle. This was about two years ago, I'm talking about. Double Dee Jay was easing everything off the peak time on Saturday night. To get a disc on his show was a thing you dreamed about. If you were a respectable vocalist working out of a local radio station, that is. Well Jingle said he went for it, said it was fine. Could I get up here and see him about the chance of slipping it into the show.'

She laughed.

'Could I use a female lead opposite Cary Grant? I was on the next bus out of Sleepy Hollow and heading for the wide open city. I didn't know at the time just how wide open the city would turn out to be. I found out, though. Brother how I found out.'

She pushed away the cherry-coloured hair where it had strayed round the side of her face. She was no longer talking to me, but staring at the opposite wall, forcing out the words as if repeating a nightmare to a psychiatrist.

'I had an appointment at the A.I.C.T. building to see Jingle the first morning after I arrived. He didn't keep me waiting, or do the big-time act. He was delighted to meet me, sure he'd heard the disc, couldn't get it out of his head. We went in his office. Would I mind if he played the disc over while I was actually in the room, so he could get a better picture in his mind of the way I actually looked when I made the recording. I did not mind. I was thrilled, Preston. I was flattered, pumped right up. I loved it. He played it over twice, and anybody could see he was really sold on it. At least anybody thought she could see that. This was the first move in Jingle's pitch. I've seen it since, as no-longer-innocent bystander, and believe me it works every time. Why not? It's a good spiel.'

Whitney Blane held out her empty glass for me to do something about it. I got up, took it from her, and went across to the table. She went on talking.

'Then he explained the system to me, just a little. If it was left to him he'd put it straight in his show that night, in Donny's Dozen if he could. But there were lots of things to be considered. The first thing was that nobody had ever heard of me. I ought to meet people, some of the big bandleaders, record company brass, and like that. The night people. Well, I didn't have to worry my pretty little head about that. Old Donny Jingle just happened to be in the neighbourhood, and it just happened he knew these people, all of them. And he would be proud to introduce me around. After all, one day he'd be able to say he helped at the birth of a great star. Oh, I tell you that man could sweet-talk a monkey out of a banana. You ever meet him?'

'Once,' I nodded.

'Well he was a real sweet talker. A sweet talking bastard. Anyway, I mustn't get ahead of the story. He said he had to make the rounds of the clubs that night as it happened, and if I liked to go with him. I needn't tell you my answer to that. He took me all right. The Cabana, the Blue Light, Otto's Grotto, everywhere that is anywhere. And did I meet people. I must have met about one half of the entertainment people in the United States that night. You have to give Donny his due. He doesn't sell a girl short. Oh, I forgot to mention something. I didn't drink in those days. Not at all. Naturally, as Donny pointed out, I couldn't move among those people drinking root beer. I drank whatever they put in front of me, just to show I was one of the crowd. I think those two or three hours were probably the happiest of my whole life. You sure about that violin?'

The remark was caustic, but there was an extra brightness in her eyes that told me she wasn't feeling so tough at that moment.

'I woke up in some lousy motel over near Fullerton. I found that things with me were not as they used to be. I cut up a bit, but Donny slapped me around a little to calm me down.' Involuntarily, a hand crept to the side of her face. 'He was addicted to a little casual slapping now and then. That, and other things. Well there I was, hooked. He was still giving me the pitch about the record, and I still wanted it. This, he told me, was the entrance. I was luckier than most of his girl-friends. I really could sing a little. So, after a while, he put me in the show. I'm really a jazz singer you know, but with the Double Dee Jay it was all pop stuff. Progressive was out. I could sing in key and keep to the melody which was all the show called for. My voice got harder. So did I. It's anybody's money which came first. After a time the bedroom bit dropped away, Donny never could concentrate on one woman for any length of time. But I was getting a little popularity of my own, all reflected, naturally. As long as I didn't get out of line I could stay on the show. Then, about six months back I found I couldn't do anything to please him at all. He'd cuss me out, and he's an expert, in front of the whole crew, within one minute of the red light. I was soon tipped off what was happening. Donny's latest chick was another singer who could hold a tune. He was looking for any excuse to get rid of me and put her in.'

I was standing beside her listening, with her fresh drink in my hand. Now she took it from me, sniffed at it suspiciously.

'You put water in this?'

'No, ma'am, no water,' I assured her.

'H'm.'

She drank half the contents, made a face, and went on.

'I knew it would only be a matter of time. I started asking around. Anybody use a slightly used vocalist, good looking, wolf-bait body, large wardrobe, with own bed? I And in came the bids. That was a sweet moment, when I found I no longer needed the Double Dee Jay, and I do mean Jingle. I went to his office and spat right in his face.'

She smiled reminiscently.

'You may not think that's a very nice thing for a lady to admit, Preston. But I'm not a lady, and I'm telling you it was the greatest satisfaction of my life. Till tonight.'

'Why not do it to him while the Double Dee Jay was actually on the screen?' I queried.

'I thought about it. It was a great temptation. But there was a snag to that. I'd never get another job in any kind of entertainment if I did that. So I did it in private, and it was delicious.'

'So that was the end of the story?'

Her eyes clouded over again.

'Not quite. Jingle had the last laugh. He always did. After I was clear of the show, and my lawyer made certain A.I.C.T. had no more claim on me, I suddenly found all the offers disappearing. Mind you, I hadn't anything on paper, but everybody seemed enthusiastic enough, but suddenly no deal. I didn't work for two months.'

'You think jingle got to these people, scared 'em off?'

'It was either that, or the offers all started out from him in the first place, just to tempt me into walking out on the Double Dee Jay. Either way the bastard had me cold.'

I nodded.

'And now?'

'Oh, I'm working again now. At a club in L.A. Six nights a week eleven till three a.m. My voice is coming back a little. I'm off that pop kick working with a modern quartet. You ought to come and hear us sometime.'

'I'd like to. Well,' I scratched my head. 'You did warn me I wouldn't be able to use what you told me. You were right.'

She grinned mischievously.

'Make some great copy wouldn't it? "Dead Star was Seducer" or maybe "Jingle Jangles Juveniles."'

When she saw I didn't smile back she stopped.

'What's the matter?'

'What's all this about a dead star?' I asked.

'Why Jingle, who else? What do you think the party's for? Here's a toast. May his soul rot in hell.'

She lifted her glass, put it down again, and looked at me.

'What are you telling me?'

'Jingle's not dead—' I began.

'You're a liar,' she hissed. 'I heard it on the radio myself.'

'It was a mistake.' I insisted, 'Jingle's car blew up, but it was Dave Chisum who was inside.'

'Liar,' but she was no longer so certain.

'Believe me, I've nothing to gain by—'

'Liar,' she screamed. 'Get out. It was on the radio, it was, it was. He's dead.'

She started beating at the sides of the chair with her fists.

'He's dead, dead, dead.'

'No,' I said firmly.

The tears were flooding down her cheeks as she flung the glass at me. Some of the brandy splashed the side of my face. I dabbed at it with a handkerchief. Whitney Blane buried her face in a cushion. I went and put a hand on her shoulder.

It was on the radio,' she protested weakly, her whole body racked with deep sobs.

I felt great.

'You leave me alone, take your dirty hands

off me. You're all the same. Pigs.'

'Look, Whitney—'

'Get out. Get out.'

And all the time the sobs and the tears continued. I didn't think I ought to leave her alone like that. No telling what she might do. I lit a cigarette and leaned against the wall watching her. Gradually, the sobs became less convulsive and her breathing not so jerky. I didn't go close for another couple of minutes, then I went softly to the side and looked down at her.

She was sleeping like a baby.

CHAPTER EIGHT

The Gloomy Sunday was a place where musicians gathered at night. Somebody once described it as an upholstered cellar and as descriptions go that was close enough.

Most of the entertainment in Monkton City is centred on Conquest Street, a lusty, bawdy concrete vein leading off the heart of town. Here are the peep shows, burlesque houses, houses, as they say, of ill-fame. Revue theatres, dance joints, bars. Step right in sucker, and be clipped by experts. You have the dough, and that's the only qualification for admission. This is the street of the wide glad hand and the big hello. While the money keeps coming.

Then, suddenly, Conquest doesn't seem so friendly any more. It becomes an avenue of turned shoulders and fast farewells. The suckers have one blessed say in all this. Once they hit Conquest they know they can kiss their money goodbye. Indeed, to watch the way they set about it, most of them practically insist on a skin-job. But one democratic privilege remains. The chump has the right to decide the manner of the shearing. It is an inviolable rule of the game. He can elect to give it to a gambler, a bar-keep, a dame. He can entrust it to a bookie, or leave it in the safe hands of a dear old man who's only parting with his share of the mine because he has to go abroad for his health. If he's in a real hurry, and wants to get rid of the wad fast, he can step into one of the side streets feeding the main stem. Here he will be obliged by a mugger, one of the brotherhood who waits in all such places for the very purpose of performing this charitable service.

Leaving aside the mugger, who is looked on by the rest of the Conquest fraternity as an unskilled trade, most of the other alternatives have one thing in common. That thing is music. You can sit in a velvet-draped booth next to an amorous blonde with hard eyes, and listen to the tinkly sound of a piano stroked by soft expert fingers. You can join the burlesque gapers, and get your sex at second-hand, to the accompaniment of a well-drilled sax section. If you're energetic, you can get right out there on the floor in some dance hall at two bits a throw, partnered by an amorous brunette whose hard eyes make you think she has a blonde sister who works the bars. In the dance-joints the music comes all shapes, pop, dixieland, hip, rock and who knows what-all.

All this music provides work for a neglected section of the community. Musicians. One of the few really uncertain professions remaining to a well-planned democracy. Conquest Street means work, and the promise of work will draw the music-makers as nothing else. At least, almost nothing else. Most of them, but by no means all, have come to realise that an intake of regular meals is very beneficial to the system. Recognised, too, that the key to those meals is work. The first foundation has almost been laid. You have to work to eat. Soon these musicians may be properly disciplined to the way of life the rest of us tolerate. Like living somewhere permanent, having more day clothes than tuxedos. They haven't made it yet, haven't cottoned to the great ideal. Only partial contributors to the capital system, most of them tote around their capital in a black leather bag. And while they certainly will work when compelled, they are fidgety people. After a few days or a few weeks, they will quit. I am talking only of the real musicians, the ones who have a private sadness. There are more of them than you realise, and their sadness, though private, is the same one.

It takes between five and fifteen years to produce an A1 first-class performer. The length of time varies according to the instrument and the aptitude of the pupil. Even at its shortest, this is a big chunk out of a man's life. At the end of it he has to decide where he's going to display this great talent, what field is best suited to ensure that the widest public can benefit. He is saddened to learn that nobody is interested in music in its pure form. At least, a few here and there. Not enough to keep him in those meals we were just talking about. To eat he has to become number nineteen first violin in some symphony orchestra and grind out Tchaikowsky, Wagner and Beethoven till it comes out of his ears. Or third trumpet in the Harris Melford College Dance Orchestra (private functions by arrangement). He can tote his oboe along to the theatre orchestra, and submit to the tyranny of a conductor whose real interest lies in the performances of the singers, with the accompaniment a bad second. Or he can wear a funny suit and perform with the Original Mad Trads.

But whatever he does to prevent his stomach from rusting, he has to keep in touch. So he singles out a place where he can be with other musicians. Where he can play if he feels like it, or talk, or just listen. Such a place was the Gloomy Sunday.

It was after one in the morning when I got there. Non-musicians are not exactly welcomed with open arms. One or two people looked at me with idle curiosity, but mostly I was ignored. The lighting was so dim I couldn't be certain whether Chrazy Chris was there or not. I leaned against a wall to let my eyes get accustomed to the gloom.

'It was way out man, till along around four. Then the johns busted into the pad, put the arm on Miff, and took away the skins, too.'

'Sad.'

'I'm speaking, dad. It was like rough. Took the milk right out of the coconut, you know?'

'Wha' hoppen?'

'Like we blew some more, but we do not jell, you know? Then this twist she says she needs five for happy money. Like we don't have five in the hat. Then she cuts up like crazy. I don't want the box wounded, so I but moved on.'

'Natch. So Red stayed with the twist?'

'*Quien sabe?*'

I was just getting engrossed in the conversation between the two characters on my right when one of them noticed me. He nudged the other one and mumbled something. They shut up like clams.

Down on the platform some interesting noise was being made by a trio consisting of trombone, guitar and cello. Only experts would have dared to try and produce any kind of sound from a combination as unlikely as that. But these guys were not only trying, they were succeeding.

'Quite a step from the Original Mad Trads, huh?'

I turned to find Chrazy Chris standing watching me.

'Oh, hullo. Yeah. I guess it is.'

'Let's park the rumbles,' he said, and led the way to a small table. When we were seated he asked, 'You want something, coffee or a drink, maybe?'

'No thanks. Anyhow I thought this place was strictly coffee only?'

He nodded.

'Sure. Guy who runs it figures liquor would only bring him trouble. He'd get the wrong crowd in, then we'd all move out. So he serves coffee. We all bring in something to like lace it, if required. Nobody minds, long as there isn't any trouble.'

He produced a small flat bottle from his coat, poured some into the cap which did double duty as a shot glass. Then he tipped it down his throat, screwed the cap carefully back into place and put the bottle away.

'You seen Whitney?' he demanded.

'I was there,' I confirmed. 'She was having a party.'

'That right? Who else was there?'

'Me. And a couple of fifths of brandy.'

'Yeah.' He sounded almost sad: 'I know

about the brandy. I've seen that girl empty a fifth in about an hour.'

'Tells me she was teetotal till a couple of years ago,' I offered.

'That what she tells you?' he replied non-committally. 'What was the party all about?'

I watched his face as I replied to catch any reaction. 'She thought Donny Jingle was dead. Figured it called for a celebration.'

A sardonic grin flitted briefly across his face.

'I'll bet. She musta had close to a fit when you wised her up.'

'She certainly didn't seem too pleased,' I acknowledged. 'Why would Jingle's death be an excuse for a party?'

'Didn't she tell you?' he demanded.

'Nothing that made much sense. Mostly she called him a lot of names. Then she cried a bit, and finally passed out.'

'Uh huh. You sure you won't try a little of this?' He drew out the bottle again and patted it.

'No thanks.'

His hands were quite steady as he held the small cup against the bottle neck and slowly tipped the pale liquid in. Then in a quick, neat movement he tossed the shot down his throat. He was good at it, no splashes, no drips. Just straight down. To get that good you have to have a lot of practice. After he screwed the little cup back on to the neck of the bottle, he looked at me shrewdly.

'What d'you make of Donny?'

'Me? What would I make of him? I've only met him twice, for a few minutes each time. He seems to be the boss, but why shouldn't he be? It's his show, I guess.'

Chris screwed up his eyes as he listened.

'And what you heard from Whit Blane, that doesn't make any difference?'

'Not by itself,' I told him. 'I've been in this business too long to start hating somebody on the say so of a hysterical girl who was half-drunk into the bargain.'

He listened solemnly.

'Fair enough. I buy that. How would you like to hear another version, only this time from a man who is also half-drunk? Who spends most of his time that way.'

'I'm a great little listener,' I assured him. 'People talk and I listen. It's my racket. Talk some.'

'All right. Say how about a cigarette?'

It was getting to have a familiar sound. As I pushed the pack over to him I muttered:

'Doesn't anybody on your show ever buy his own?'

'Huh?'

'Nothing. Let's hear the story.'

'Sure. You probably wonder what I'm doing here in this place. The Gloomy Sunday is strictly for musicians, did you know that?'

104

'I knew it,' I confirmed.

'So you probably wonder how I qualify. Me, Chrazy Chris, in person. The original comic clarinet lead with the Original Mad Trads. The one with the funny hat. What makes a musical clown like that think he has any right to mix around with the real kind, do you suppose? You heard the band?'

He was talking about the Trads.

'I've heard it. You want to know if I like it, the answer is no.'

He grinned.

'Why not? We're big in Witchita, ask jingle.'

'Everybody likes what he likes. I'll take Brubeck.'

'Somebody mentioned Dave?'

A short skinny guy who'd been passing the table stopped and looked at us.

'I heard mention of the man,' he said. 'Who's your friend, Chris?'

'Hi, Art. This is Preston. He blows not, but hath an ear.'

'Well, skin.'

Art stuck out his hand and I shook it.

'Just gonna put the lungs to work,' Art announced.

'You, Chris?'

'Well, just a couple.'

Chris leaned under the table and pulled out a slim black oblong box. He snapped the catches, and when he raised the lid I could see the two halves of an ebony clarinet, nestled against blue velvet. He raised the two pieces lovingly and fitted them together. Then he took a mouth-piece from a small compartment in a corner of the box and screwed this carefully home. Finally he took another small box from the handkerchief pocket of his jacket and began to sort through a couple of dozen reeds.

'Have to watch your reeds,' he told me. 'You pick the wrong one, the little beauty'll split on you right in the middle of a chorus.'

Art chuckled.

'These reed-men,' he scoffed. 'Real mother hens. I've seen 'em practically bust out cryin' when an old favourite split.'

'I thought they were mostly made of plastic these days,' I chipped in.

Art sighed, while Chris looked at me stonily.

'Well, that's what happens when you let the peasants in,' Art told him. 'They're liable to make cracks like that.'

It seemed to be time for me to stop talking. Chris was finally satisfied with his instrument.

'Don't go away, Preston,' he said, getting up from the table. 'Just be a few minutes, honest. Make me feel better.'

He and Art sauntered over to the stand, and stood listening to the trio. Art reached behind an empty chair and came up with a glittering, gold-lacquered trumpet. He stood, breathing softly into it to warm it up. The trio reached the end of the number and turned to say hello to the newcomers. I moved over to Chris's vacant seat to get a better view of what was going on. He and Art found seats on the platform and the guitar-man eased the group in with some intricate four-four harmonics. At the end of four bars the rest of the musicians came in, Art leading. I'd had enough practice at listening to know it was 'Foggy Day' they were playing. It was an experience to hear them. They had no score, and had soon left the original chord-sequence way behind, yet each man played with this instinctive understanding of what everybody else in the group was doing. I was especially interested in Chris. All I'd ever heard from him was a squeaky, unimaginative lead on things like 'Saints' and 'Bugle Call'. The usual repertoire of the high school dance-band, now translated to the big-money brackets by the adroit manipulations of the ad-men who had sold the young and musically illiterate the notion that this was real jazz. Chris was one of the national heroes of this brigade, with his faithful copies of old Chicago and New Orleans groups. It had never occurred to me that maybe the guy could really play. It occurred to me now. It was noticeably quieter in the Gloomy Sunday as the group warmed to the number. And when the musicians listen, you can be sure there's something worth hearing. There was not much solo work, the wind instruments taking it in turn to lead while everyone else improvised all round the soloist. The effect was that of an intricate sound-pattern, never still, almost ethereal in its elusive refusal to linger.

They played four choruses of 'Foggy Day' and as the last notes died away, I began to clap my hands. Everybody turned to identify the moron. The moron stopped clapping. Chris came back alone, stripped down the clarinet and packed it away.

'Where d'you think you are, Radio City Music Hall?' he snapped irritably.

'Sorry,' I mumbled.

'Ah, forget it. Anyway, you musta liked it,' he sounded more cheerful.

'Liked is hardly adequate,' I assured him. 'Why don't you guys record stuff like that?'

'It's been tried, still is occasionally. Somebody makes a disc worth hearing now and then. Nobody buys it, natch. Anyway you were lucky tonight. The cello-man is the most. He just stayed over for twenty-four hours on his way to Australia. Got a big concert tour coming up. That's Alberto Santini.'

I looked over at the famous soloist, now happily plugging away at 'Take Five'.

'All right, so I'm a tourist,' I admitted. 'But I didn't come here to talk about music. When I talk about music, I wouldn't have the nerve to do it in company like this. Murder is my racket, remember?'

'I remember.'

He took another of my Old Favourites, lit it,

and let a hazy cloud of grey smoke filter from his nostrils.

'I can play, no?'

'You can play, yes. But it hasn't anything to do—'

'You're wrong,' he interrupted. 'It has everything to do with it. One of the main reasons I got up there just now was so you'd hear me. It'll help you understand what I have to tell you.'

'All right, go ahead.'

'I'm a pro musician. You now know the way I play. Nobody needs it, but they need other kinds of music. I play it, so that they pay me enough dough to keep me healthy enough to play what they don't want. Make sense?'

'Vaguely.'

'Couple of years ago I was looking for work. I'd been on the Squareville tour—'

I held up a hand.

'Please keep the language so that I can follow.'

'Oh, sure. A squareville tour is where a name band hits the road and works itself nearly to death doing one-night stands in any town that's big enough to fill a hall.'

'Thank you. You'd just finished such a tour. Then what?'

'I was loafing around, doing an occasional tee-vee commercial, stuff like that when my agent told me A.I.C.T. was looking for a band for the Double Dee Jay. They were changing the format a little. Every six weeks they wanted a different band. This was going to be a novelty group. Few guys blowing real crude 1920s stuff. Le Jazz Hot. You know. So I scraped up the guys, told 'em it would be a lot of laughs, and it was just a few weeks of big eating money. We all thought it was a great big joke. We were right too, only it wasn't us did the laughing. It was Witchita.'

'I remember the Trads were a big hit,' I recalled.

'You got the word,' he assented. 'I didn't mind. Like I say it was a lotta fun. Then we got near the end of our stretch. We thought. I asked Jingle who was putting in the new group and he said what new group. I reminded him we were only sentenced to six weeks, and he told me my agent had signed a new deal for me. More money, extended indefinite contract. I saw the agent. He'd sold me out completely. Any options in the contract were all on Jingle's side. I went to lawyers, they all came up with the same answer. I was stuck. Jingle had my agent put out the word. I threatened to walk, and you know what? The Union called me in. Told me they'd been into it, and if I walked out on the show I might lose my card. They couldn't see what I was complaining about. Nobody could. And of course the card bit screwed me right down. Without a card I couldn't even play at the brakemen's stag.'

'And you've been on the show ever since,' I finished.

'Bet. You must think I'm crazy, complaining about a fat steady job like that. Maybe I am, but I'm a freelance, Preston. Guys like me don't go for that pension thing.'

'You blame Jingle, I notice. Not the network.'

'Right. It was Jingle, he told me so. He tells me so every time he feels like it. He tells everybody just where they fit in, all the time. He's a man with a real nice disposition. The happy family gag at Double Dee Jay is one of the biggest frauds ever put across old joe public. There isn't a soul on the show doesn't hate Jingle's guts.'

'Enough to put a bomb in his car?' I queried.

'Why not? Done it myself if I had the nerve.'

'And did you?'

He laughed.

'You're a cool guy, Preston. No, I didn't. Sorry about Dave though, he was on the level. Whoever got him instead of Donny must be feeling like hell.'

His tone was sincere, and I didn't get the impression he was merely saying the right thing about Chisum.

'Whitney Blane was feeling like hell when I left her,' I remarked. 'Not because Chisum was dead, but because Jingle wasn't.'

'I imagine. You'd seen the way that pig used

to treat the poor kid, you'd understand.'

'She ever lose her temper?'

'Now and then. You're asking me what she was like when she got mad, aren't you? Could she kill somebody? I don't know about just anybody, but Jingle yes. When she had a good mad on she could have hacked him up with a meat cleaver. But putting the big firework in a car, that's a different kind of mood, isn't it? She could have done it, I guess. Any of us could. But I wouldn't have thought she could be that cold-blooded.'

'Maybe. Tell me about Chisum. Why'd he stick?'

'He started out with Jingle, back in Jerkwater, Idaho or such. Why he stuck was for the money, plus the fact Jingle would see to it he didn't work anywhere else once he quit. And his wife is a spender. She wouldn't sit easy on a carhop's pay, which is about what Dave would get outside this racket.'

'How did Jingle treat him?'

'Same as everybody else. None of that old buddy-buddy stuff for Jingle. He's such a big man, he probably figured it was a special privilege for Dave to know him longer than the rest of us. Loyalty is not a word Donny knows much about.'

'He seemed to be doing as he was told while Kingworth was around,' I prompted.

'Kingworth? Oh sure, our beloved vice-president. Yeah, Donny behaves himself with

Kingworth. That man is very tough indeed. And he's got religion.'

Religion was not something I would have associated with the fat man. He wasn't the type to accept easily the notion of an authority higher than his own.

'I didn't get the impression he was a religious man,' I said.

Chris twisted his face in a smile.

'Then you weren't paying attention. Kingworth worships the buck. The network is his church, and joe public is his congregation. Anybody does anything sacrilegious, something that might affect the take, winds up outside the temple.'

He relapsed into moody silence.

'Hey, Chris.'

We turned to see Art walking towards us, the golden trumpet gleaming richly in his hand.

'The guys want to try something that needs a stick-man. And you're the only one here. Come and blow.'

'Right with you.'

Art went away and the clarinet player turned back to me.

'Mind if I split the scene? I told you what I wanted you to know. About Donny, I mean.'

'Sure. Before you go, you couldn't possibly think of just one single thing that might put me on this guy's tail? I mean the killer.'

He shook his head, and the smile he gave

me was not pleasant.

'You musta blown your stack, man. I can't think of one single thing, no. But I can think of about fifty. And I'm not going to tell you a single one of 'em. Sure I'm sorry about Dave, but what's done is done. Next time the guy'll get Donny good, and make it stick. You think I'm going to tell you anything that might stop him you're crazy. Not me, nor anybody else on the show. Be seeing you.'

He rose and went to rejoin the group on the stand. As I left the Gloomy Sunday, the mournful notes of a low-register clarinet mocked me into the night.

CHAPTER NINE

It was three in the morning when I opened the door of my apartment. Gil Randall was parked in one of my chairs, half asleep.

'Nice hours you keep,' he grumbled.

'I didn't think you'd wait up, mama,' I told him sourly. 'Does it ever cross your mind that maybe some people don't like to find other people in their private homes. Even police people?'

He stirred sluggishly in the chair. It was a good-sized chair but Randall overflowed in all directions. He's a big man, seventy four inches from the ground and two hundred pounds of

114

trained muscle packed into a solid frame. His features are not what you would call alert, and a lot of people get a first impression that this is the dumb flatfoot they read about. The guilty ones sometimes even make the mistake of acting on that initial impression, and when they do they've taken their first step towards that small room with the bars on the windows.

'Now don't get all citizen-fashion on me, Preston. It's been a rough night as it is. Besides, I came here to do you a favour.'

I sniffed.

'Don't let me stop you.'

'There you go again,' he complained. 'Listen, what do you make of this bomb deal?'

'Thought you came here to do something for me? Is this the favour, helping me unburden my mind of anything I may know that you don't?'

'First things first. Well?'

'I don't know. It's screwy. Everybody mixed up in the Double Dee Jay also seems screwy to me. You?'

He pursed his lips.

'A man is dead. That is not screwy, Preston. That is murder. And premeditated, leave us not forget.'

'It was not premeditated that Chisum should collect the blast,' I objected.

'Makes no difference in law. Nor in a moral argument even. To kill somebody without even having a reason, nobody could defend that.'

'All right, Gil. I don't want to argue. I don't even want to agree. What I want is sleep.'

'Me too. Who do you think would want to kill this Donny Jingle? My family catch the show most Saturdays. Seems to be a nice enough feller.'

With Randall, if you know him, it pays to think before you say too much. I knew him.

'All I have is hearsay and rumour, Gil,' I hedged.

He spread his large hands and grinned.

'Go ahead, spread a little scandal. Gossip some. Maybe I'll lend you some flour like a good little neighbour.'

'I've been hearing the same things as you, I imagine. Jingle is a four-flusher, a chaser, a take-artist. An all-American heel, so they tell me. I'll say that again. That's what they tell me. What I know is nothing.'

'So?'

'So they tell me he could have been shot at by half the people in California, all with very good reasons. They also tell me the chance of the police getting much in the way of co-operation in finding the killer is not strong. From what I hear, everybody hopes the guy will try again, and have better luck. There was even a mention that a public subscription should be raised if he does make it.'

'Uh huh,' he seemed satisfied. 'That about ties in with what we hear. If what we have about this Jingle is true, or even half of it, the guy certainly deserves to get hit. Unfortunately, the taxpayers in this town don't pay the department to pass judgments. Just to uphold the law. So we can't let this killer walk around. We got to pick him up.'

'Make that a lot easier if you knew who it was, wouldn't it?'

I couldn't resist that.

Randall didn't bat an eye as he said:

'Oh, we know who it was. We're dragging the town now.'

Ten seconds earlier I'd have sworn I was tired. I was wrong. Trying to keep the eagerness out of my voice I asked,

'Will you get court-martialled or something if you tell me?'

'I'll take a chance. It was the little guy, Shoeman.'

'Mo?'

A picture of that india-rubber face, with the frowns on top and the smiles on the lower half flashed across my mind.

'You're sure about this?'

'We'll have to be a little surer before we lock him in the gas-chamber, but he's good, he's very good. We don't put a man on the wires at two in the morning just to be sure everybody's awake.'

I knew that was true. If John Rourke had elected Shoeman he had plenty of good reason.

'What made it Shoeman?'

'Three things. First he hates Jingle's guts. You say, so does everybody in town, but Shoeman has reasons for two people. Himself, because of the way he gets kicked around from breakfast to bedtime. And somebody else, somebody who gives him a much stronger motive. You remember the singer used to be on the Double Dee Jay, Whitney Blane?'

'I remember.'

'Shoeman's sister. There's a big age-gap, the mother produced the girl late in life. Soon after, the parents were killed in a road accident. Shoeman's been more like a father than a brother. She was a nice kid, I hear. Jingle, the people's choice, turned her into a lush and worse.'

I wasn't altogether convinced.

'I can see why a man with that provocation would kill somebody. But he's left it a long time before he did anything about it, hasn't he? Why, do you suppose?'

Randall sighed and ran a hand through the crisp black hair.

'I don't suppose anything. I gave up supposing about people ten years ago. One thing you learn in this job. The longer you do it, the less you can predict what people will do. I stick to facts.'

'You said three things pointed to him. What about the other two?'

'The bomb,' he replied. 'Suppose you wanted to get rid of somebody with a bomb.

How'd you go about it?'

I thought.

'I don't know. Bombs are a mystery to me. I mean about really making one. I know enough to snuff a fuse if I see one smoking.'

'Sure,' he agreed. 'That's what you know about bombs. Unlike poison. A kid of eight years old could tell you. But bombs you have to know.'

'And Mr. Shoeman knows,' I finished.

'He does. Worked three years in a munitions factory one time. Been in most of the departments. Knows assembly of most types of hand-bomb backwards. Nobody else in this knows any more than you know. Most of 'em don't even know about the fuse.'

'Sounds bad,' I admitted. 'What's your third point?'

'Easy. The guy's gone. After we got through with our little talk at the offices there, Shoeman walked out the front door and vanished.'

'But he could have gone for a drink somewhere, visited some dame. Anything like that. It's only a few hours back.'

'Yeah. He could have. But we haven't been able to dig him up so far. And we're trying.'

I felt sorry about Shoeman. Mostly I haven't any feelings about murderers, but Shoeman was different. A man who'd been pushed around all his life, that much was written on his face. Finally he got to a corner where he turned and hit back. With good reason, too. Reasons which a smart lawyer would use to keep him free of the maximum penalty. But when he hit back, he fluffed. He couldn't even kill somebody efficiently. He got the wrong man. For that he'd have to pay, and rightly. But I was sorry about it.

'Thanks for letting me know, Gil. I appreciate the favour.'

'That wasn't it,' he retorted.

'Huh?'

My puzzlement was genuine.

'Something else. We had a guy come forward after he caught the late news, the bit about the dead man being Chisum and not Jingle. This guy said Chisum called at his place earlier tonight.'

I felt an uneasiness somewhere below my chest.

'The taxpayer works at the *Bulletin*. According to him Chisum was round there in the early evening rooting around in the morgue. He described him. The description didn't fit Chisum at all, but it sounded a helluva lot like you. Your ball.'

'It was me,' I nodded. 'You see—'

'I know, I know. There was no way of knowing what was going to happen later. You knew Chisum wouldn't mind. You knew some reporter would recognise your own name, smell a story, and check on what files you looked at. So you wrote Chisum. It was lucky for you the information got to Rourke before Durrant saw it. The Assistant Commissioner wants everything on this case brought to his personal notice. And he can be very irritable at times. So the lieutenant forgot to pass this on. He doesn't think it has a bearing. Now, you tell me the lieutenant is right, and we can all get some sleep.'

I told Randall what I'd been looking for at the *Bulletin*. He asked me a few questions, but was satisfied finally. We chatted a few minutes more, and I said I'd call him the next morning to find out how the search on Shoeman was coming. After that he left.

My new-found awakeness went with him. Ten minutes after the door closed I was in bed.

*   *   *

Something was buzzing in my head and I knew I ought to be doing something about it. I didn't. The buzzing went on, became louder and shriller as it penetrated gradually through the sleep-fog. It was almost like a bell. All right, it was a bell. Telephone. I muttered a phrase I picked up in the navy and burrowed deeper into the pillow. It wasn't any use. My ears had now tuned in fully to the unmelodious jangle. Reluctantly I reached out and lifted the thing up. As my left wrist moved across my squinting eyes I got a quick flash of the watch dial. It seemed to point to ten minutes after seven. That had to be wrong of course. I looked again. It was not wrong. As I lay wondering who there could be in the world with so much hatred in him that he'd get me out of bed after less than four hours' sleep. An anxious hallo, hallo, kept repeating from the instrument in my hand.

'Well?' I mumbled.

'Is that Mr. Preston, the Mark Preston they're talking about in the papers this morning?'

It was a woman's voice, shrill and unattractive.

'I don't know,' I told her. 'I haven't seen any papers yet. What do they say about me?'

'Not much. It's this man who was murdered last night, this Mr. Chisum. Says right there you're one of these private investigators and you're working for the video people.'

'If it says that, it's correct. Was that all you wanted to know? Who is this anyway?'

'I'll tell you that later,' she replied. She seemed to be trying to keep her voice down, as though to be sure nobody at her end could hear what she said. But its natural pitch was so piercing I doubted whether she was having much luck. 'Listen, I think I know something about all this.'

'Then go to the police,' I advised. 'They always welcome information.'

'I've already told them what I know,' she surprised me.

'But at the time I didn't know it had any connection with video or like that. Now I think it does, I heard you people might pay me to give an exclusive story to the newspapers.'

'If the police have it already,' I told her, 'they don't make deals with single newspapers. They either keep quiet about it or tell all the newspapers at the same time.'

'Wait, wait,' she spoke quickly. 'It's about another crime, something else the police are working on. I'm the only connection between that one and this murder. The police don't realise it yet. Or, if they do, they haven't been round to see me.'

I thought about it. It was probably nothing. I needed more sleep. This dame was probably all wrong. I said:

'Look, I can't make any kind of deal by myself. I'll get in touch with a newspaper and see if they're interested. Will you call me back in ten minutes?'

'You think they will? How much will I get?'

'Ten minutes,' I repeated sourly, and broke the connection. Then I got through to the *Monkton City Globe*. I was lucky. The day editor this week was Shad Steiner. I told him the story. Like me, he wasn't wild about it.

'Preston,' he said wearily; 'I get most of twenty people a week want to sell me exclusive information. It usually works out they don't know anything at all. If they know something, I can't use it because they ought to be calling the police, not me.'

'I know, Shad, but can we afford not even bothering to find out what it's all about?'

There was a pause.

'All right, all right. This is my quiet time, now till around eight-thirty. Get the secret surprise witness here as fast as you can. I hope you're not wasting my time.'

'Your time?' I snorted. 'Listen, I haven't had any sleep yet.'

I paddled out and warmed over some coffee. While I was doing it she called back. I explained the situation to her.

'At the *Globe* office,' she repeated doubtfully. 'Listen, how do I know I can trust them, or you? You might get my story then not pay me.'

'Suit yourself,' I snapped. 'It was your idea to get in touch.'

'Well, all right. I guess I'll be there.'

'Twenty minutes.'

At seven forty-five I walked into Shad Steiner's office. He was sorting through a wad of paper, placing the sheets in one of three separate piles in trays marked 'Immediate', 'Fill' and 'Reject'.

'Well, well,' he greeted. 'The Sherlock Holmes of the side-streets. Don't believe I've seen you around at this hour of the day before.'

'You haven't,' I assured him.

'You won't mind if I just get on with some of

these unimportant news items here? Naturally, I've left word to stop the presses when the big story breaks.'

I parked in a corner and waited. Not long. At seven-fifty a copy-boy poked his head in the door.

'There's a woman outside says she has an appointment. Won't tell me her name.'

Shad looked across at me.

'Her name is Mata Hari,' he said. 'Let her in.'

Any resemblance to Mata Hari was lost on me when she came in. She was short and scraggy, with a pinched face, and sharp little button eyes. She could be anything between forty and sixty.

'Come in and sit down please. My name is Steiner, I'm the editor, and this is Mr. Preston whom you talked to on the telephone.'

She nodded, licked her lips, and perched awkwardly on a high-backed chair. I nodded at her encouragingly.

'Listen,' and the voice was even shriller close to, 'Listen, I don't want to do nothing wrong. Nothing against the law, that is.'

'Don't worry, madam,' Shad assured her. 'You won't break any laws with the connivance of this paper. If you ought to be with the authorities I shall advise you to go there when I've heard your story.'

She kept the button eyes on his face as he spoke. Her head bobbed quickly.

125

'I'm Mrs. Monahan,' she announced. 'I was in all the papers just last week. The Colfax case.'

'Yes, yes, I remember,' said Shad. 'You were witness at the inquest.'

She bobbed her head again.

'The only witness,' she emphasised importantly.

I looked at her with new interest. The week previously, a nineteen year old girl named Ellie Colfax had committed suicide in a cheap apartment house in the Harbour area. It wasn't an important case, and there was no angle to it the papers could play on. The girl wasn't in any kind of trouble. She'd arrived in Monkton a couple of days earlier, taken this room. She didn't get a job, didn't seem to know anybody. Then she bought some sleeping pills, took an overdose and died. It could even have been a mistake, the medical examiner pointed out at the inquest. There was no reason why this young attractive girl should take her I own life. But the Coroner's jury had decided on a suicide verdict, and the world settled down to forget Ellie Colfax. The only bit of excitement at the hearing was the testimony of the woman in the apartment below, Mrs. Monahan. She had seen a man leaving the building the afternoon before Ellie died. She couldn't be certain he'd been visiting the dead girl, but she did know he wasn't a tenant. The police tried to find the man, on the meagre description supplied by Mrs. Monahan, but had no success. It was all pretty vague, and in any case there was no suggestion the man was the last person to see her alive. The same evening, Ellie had been down to a supermarket to pick up some cigarettes.

'I guess you remember all about poor Ellie Colfax,' prompted Mrs. Monahan.

'Certainly, Mrs. Monahan,' beamed Steiner. 'I remember especially your evidence about the visitor she had, the man the police couldn't locate.'

She sniffed.

'Couldn't locate, he says. Couldn't be bothered with, if you ask me.'

Mrs. Monahan was evidently not pleased with the police. There she was, the only person able to identify the mysterious stranger, and the police couldn't find him. It isn't every day the average citizen gets involved in front-page news, and it is liable to give him or her a distorted outlook when it happens. I could see what had been in her mind. The dramatic courtroom bit, the accusing finger of the upright, unimpeachable witness. 'That is the man.' Just like on the movies. Except that the man, even if he had visited the Colfax girl, certainly had not killed her. The police knew that much. Then again, the description they had from Mrs. Monahan was not much help. They didn't manage to turn up the man, and once the coroner's jury pronounced its verdict, they forgot about him. So did everyone else. Except Mrs. Monahan.

'Suppose I've found him,' she snapped. 'Found this brute who drove that poor girl to her death. What would you pay me? No, wait. Suppose I told you the same man was one of the people mixed up in this here murder last night?'

'And are you telling us that, Mrs. Monahan?' queried Steiner.

'I am,' she replied.

'I would be interested, naturally,' he opened cautiously. 'But I don't know that I'm sure it'll be of very much importance. After all, there was no suggestion this man killed that unfortunate girl. The police were quite satisfied about that point before they dropped the search.'

'He was a man, wasn't he? I know the way they can treat a woman, make her wish she was dead.'

We wouldn't make much progress if we let this sharp little creature get off on an anti-male campaign.

'Mrs. Monahan,' I said, in my best wheedling voice, 'Let me assure you I selected this newspaper out of all those in town, because of Mr. Steiner's reputation. If your story has any value to it from a news angle, I can assure you the *Globe* will pay. And a better price than you'd I get elsewhere.'

As I spoke I was conscious of Steiner's eyes

boring into me, begging me not to be so generous with his money. But he said nothing.

'Well O.K. if you say so, Mr. Preston,' she was mollified. 'I guess it's all right.'

'I'm sure it will be,' I repeated. 'Now, who was this man?'

'The dead one. The one got blown up. Mr. Chisum.'

So even if she were right, and it had been Chisum visiting the Colfax girl, we were on a dead lead from the beginning. Shad Steiner said:

'What makes you so positive, Mrs. Monahan?'

'Positive?' she derided. 'Wasn't it me saw that murdering brute's face, not one minute after he left that defenceless girl? Wasn't it me shivering with fright every night in my apartment in case he came back to get rid of the only witness? What makes me positive, he says. Let me tell you, Mr. Schneider, I'll take that man's face to my grave.'

'It's Steiner,' he corrected gently. 'Well, even supposing you are right, I don't see that we can do much with the story now, Mrs. Monahan. The girl is dead, so is Mr. Chisum. I can't see there'd be much point to raking over a suicide just for the doubtful satisfaction of involving a man who's since died himself. However,' he hastened on, seeing that she was about to explode, 'I will put my very best man on to it. Get him to enquire into Chisum's private affairs. Find out what the connection was between him and Miss Colfax. If there is a story we may or may not decide to print it. But I will personally guarantee you get paid either way. On one condition.'

'What's that?'

'I have to have your word that you won't discuss the matter with anyone else at all. Not even your family or friends. Certainly you must not go to another newspaper, or it's no deal. And in case you thought about the possibility of getting two papers bidding against each other for the story, I ought to warn you that all the papers in this area have an agreement. If anybody tries a stunt like that, all the papers have agreed not to print anything at all.'

He'd been close to the mark there, I suspected. Mrs. Monahan was looking a little crestfallen.

'How much do I get?' she enquired.

'That will depend on what my man finds out. If it's good you'll get a good price, as I've promised.'

'You think it's O.K., Mr. Preston?' she turned to me.

'I'm sure of it, or I wouldn't have brought you here.'

'Well, I guess so, then.' She accepted reluctantly, stood up and got ready to leave. 'When will I know?'

'By tomorrow certainly,' replied Shad. 'Possibly sooner. Could you call the office this evening, about seven?'

She agreed that she could, and left. Steiner gave her a minute to get clear then said to me:

'What d'you think?'

I shrugged.

'I don't know. I think I agree with what you said just now. No point in stirring up a lot of mud about Dave Chisum and the dead girl. The only person to suffer will be his widow.'

He frowned thoughtfully.

'I shouldn't waste too many tears on that lady. When the police called to break the news last night, they had to wait at the apartment an hour before her boy-friend brought her home. As to just ordinary mud, you're right. But I'd like to know whether that's the case. Whether there isn't something else here we should know about.' Raising his voice to a bellow he shouted:

'Copy-boy.'

Quickly the door opened and a youth bounded in.

'Mr. Steiner?'

'I want the file on that Colfax suicide last week. And all the stuff on the Double Dee Jay crowd.'

'First one's easy, Mr. Steiner, but Ed's working on a spread for tomorrow on the video story.'

'Really?' Steiner smiled dangerously. 'I don't care if Ed is writing the great American novel, I want that stuff in here, all of it. And

Ed, too,' he shouted at the retreating figure.

'What'd you make of our lady witness?' he asked me.

'Vindictive old bat,' I replied. 'She probably couldn't identify Dave Chisum on oath. Just can't bear to have the limelight suddenly switched off, like it was after the inquest.'

'Vindictive, yes,' he agreed. 'Scarcely impartial, was she? But I've a hunch she was telling the truth. I also have another hunch, that you may have brought me a bigger story than you know.'

While we waited for the papers I said:

'That was interesting that bit you told her about having an agreement with the other newspapers. I didn't know that before.'

'Ah,' his eyes twinkled. 'Then you learned about it at the same time as me. At least two papers in this town would be glad of a chance to price the *Globe* out of this story. But I thought if the lady was given an impression she might not get paid by any of us, it would seal her lips tighter than any of that honour bright stuff.'

I grinned.

'You're in the wrong business, Mr. Schneider.'

'Maybe you're right. Mr. Petfood.'

The copy-boy came in at the rush, carrying a slim brown folder.

'Not much on Colfax, Mr. Steiner. Ed's bringing the Double Dee Jay.'

132

Steiner nodded and took the folder. There were only three clippings. The first was a report on the discovery of the body. As the cause of death was unknown at that stage, there were two columns and a picture. Then there was a single column on the coroner's inquest, and last a half-inch report on the funeral.

I looked at the picture. Ellie Colfax was a pretty kid, with wide set eyes and strong cheekbones. Rustic, but pretty. Shad was reading it with me.

'There it is.'

His finger stabbed suddenly at a point halfway down the first column of the death report. I looked over his shoulder and read:

. . . arrived a few days ago from Lakecrest, Nevada. Her sorrowing parents know of no reason why she should have . . .

I read it again, then a third time. Steiner waited.

'Have you got it, yet?'

I hadn't quite. Something was niggling at the back of my mind but I hadn't brought it into focus as Ed Lorrimer walked in, weighed down with a thick bundle of files.

'You wanted all of it, S.S.,' he greeted, as he dumped the stuff in front of his editor. 'Hi, Preston.'

'Morning Ed, how are the boys?'

133

Lorrimer has two sons, and the mildest enquiry can normally produce a twenty-minute pocket history on their progress, medical, school-wise, social etc. But with Steiner there I ought to be safe.

'Fine, just fine, thanks,' he returned.

Steiner sorted through the heap rapidly, finally found what he wanted, turned to the beginning and read. Even as he handed it over, I suddenly remembered what I'd been struggling for. He was pointing to a small clippping about a Donny Jingle show early in his Monkton days. It was a fairly complimentary review about being wildly enthusiastic. The bit we were interested in read,

'. . . who hit Monkton a month ago, with his associate, Dave Chisum. These two have been making quite a mark in local radio around Vegas, and now it looks . . .'

I nodded.

'Yes, I was gradually waking up. What d'you think, Shad?'

He had the telephone in his hand and was speaking.

'I want to know the name of the paper in Lakecrest, Nevada, then the editor's name. When you have that, get him for me, will you?' Then, to me, 'Maybe nothing. Or maybe a big beautiful something.'

134

'Is it a big beautiful secret?' enquired Lorrimer.

'No,' replied his boss. Then he told the reporter what we had.

'H'm,' mused Ed, at the end. 'And now you're thinking this girl Colfax came from Lakecrest, and Donny Jingle used to operate from that station once. And that he may have known this girl back in those days. I can follow all that, but so what? It was all a long time ago wasn't it?'

'Yes, Ed,' said Steiner patiently. 'It was all a long time ago till Ellie Colfax came to Monkton and died. That brings it up to last week. Now Chisum's dead. That was last night. What was a long time ago suddenly becomes here and now. Or seems to.'

The phone rang.

'Steiner,' he rapped, 'Franklyn-Yeah-*Lakecrest Bugle,* yeah—any motto?—oh no—well thanks. The call is on the way huh?'

He replaced the receiver, took a thick book from the shelf behind him and riffled through.

'Here it is, Lakecrest, pop. 18,000. It's forty miles west of Vegas, practically on the state line. There's an airstrip.'

The phone jangled again.

'Hullo. Am I speaking to Mr. Josh Franklyn, the editor? How do you do, sir, my name is Steiner, I'm editor of the *Monkton City Globe.*'

He winked at me solemnly, while the man at the other end said his piece.

135

'No, Mr. Franklyn, the honour is all mine, sir. The *Bugle* has a fine record for living up to its motto, The Truth First and Last eh?'

Steiner drivelled on for a while, finally got round to Ellie Colfax. His voice dropped confidentially.

'Mr. Franklyn I happen to know there are still one or two loose ends connected with this unfortunate girl's death. Can you tell me from your files whether she's had any publicity in the past—well naturally, strictest confidence on both sides I hope—I see. Is that a fact, sir?—no, no but it isn't in my hands, you realise—quite. Look, Mr. Franklyn, I'm very grateful for what you've told me. Now let me return the favour. I happen to know there's a special deputy coming to Lakecrest, may even arrive this morning. If I send one of my men along with him, you think the chief would let him listen in?—you don't tell me? Well it sounds great—sure, I'll see to it myself you have all the facts. This is going to be a scoop for the *Globe*, and you have my personal assurance, sir, that the *Lakecrest Bugle* will publish the story on the same day. Absolutely—'

There was more of the same, back and forth. Finally Steiner let loose with a few more high-sounding phrases and put the phone down.

'We're in business,' he observed softly.

'Great, but what kind of business? What was

it all about, and how do you know about this special deputy?' I asked.

'Wait, wait,' he was picking up the phone again. 'I want a private charter aircraft waiting to leave in twenty minutes. Don't take any stall, even if they put the bite on us for extra money. Just get it. Two passengers. And get me the mayor's office.'

Steiner rubbed his hands together with glee.

'I haven't had so much fun in years. My smeller tells me this is a big one, and Lord help me if I'm wrong. Charter airplanes, yet.'

Lorrimer and I exchanged puzzled looks.

'Ed, this is your lucky day. You just happen to be the guy doing the paint job on the Double Dee Jay story, and that puts you in this. I can't afford to have half the paper know about it.'

'Thanks, S.S.,' replied Lorrimer. 'But just what is it I'm in on?'

That was what I was wondering, too. I knew what the call to the mayor's office was for. Since the big scandal of twenty years before, the time half the city administration wound up in the penitentiary, the mayor's office had the right to appoint special deputies at any time. The right was seldom exercised, and then mostly as a kind of civic honour, but nevertheless a special deputy had powers, with the mayor's direct authority, to make investigations, and represent the mayor in a number of ways.

Steiner still hadn't answered Lorrimer's question. He was tapping at the clipping in front of him, and concentrating.

'This girl Colfax was raped, as a minor. She was fifteen years and ten months old at the time. It was three and a half years back and they never caught the man. I'm crazy, if you like, but I've been a newshound more years than either of you has been alive, and I say there's something here.'

'You mean you think this Chisum—?' began Lorrimer.

'I don't think anything at all,' snapped Steiner. 'I'm not at the thinking stage. Just smelling. And I smell copy here. Big four-inch headline copy. You guys are going to get it for me.'

'Guys?' I queried. 'Where do I come in this?'

The damned phone rang again.

'Steiner. You did? Good. What about the other call—oh, O.K. Just a minute.'

He clapped a hand over the mouthpiece and looked at us.

'Boys, I want to have a few private words with a friend of mine. If you'll just step out in the corridor and have a smoke? I won't be long.'

We went out, closing the door carefully. Lorrimer took one of my Old Favourites and snapped a gold lighter.

'If it was anybody else but Shad I'd say we

were witnesses to a brainstorm,' he muttered.

'I agree, but I have a healthy respect for his judgment,' I replied.

'You do the right thing,' he confirmed. 'I've never seen him flip like this.'

I flicked ash on the floor.

'Looks as though we might be travelling companions on a little trip.'

'Yeah,' he agreed morosely. 'First time I've ever been sent out on a private airplane story, and what do I draw? Lakecrest, Nevada. Personally, I don't believe there is such a place.'

'Oh but there is,' I assured him. 'Practically on the state line. Population 18,000.'

A bellow from the office behind told us we could go back in. Steiner beamed widely, and tossed something at me. I caught it, and found myself holding a silver shield about two inches deep. It bore the inscription 'Special Deputy, Mayor's Office, Monkton City, Cal.'

'Sit down, Deputy Preston. You too, Ed.'

I did as I was told. I was not in shape to resist Steiner at pressure, after only four hours' sleep.

'How'd you get this hunk of tin?'

Shad continued to beam.

'Little professional secret, Preston. The power of the press, you must have heard of it. If not, you could say blackmail.'

'Blackmail I like better,' I retorted. 'Listen, I work for A.I.C.T. I'm due there at ten this morning. I can't just go gallivanting off to Horseville, Nebraska, or wherever. Besides what is Rourke gonna do to me, when he finds out about this badge?'

'If he has any sense, he'll try to persuade you to tell him what you found out. As for A.I.C.T., I'll fix them. Now, let's get down to it. We haven't much time.'

Steiner talked and we listened. There were some questions and answers back and forth. After that I put in my call to Randall about my trip.

At nine o'clock, Lorrimer and I were wedged in a light aircraft, taxiing into the wind at Monkton Airport.

CHAPTER TEN

Within an hour we were out over mountain and desert country on a north-east heading. Looking down at the blistered ground and those uncompromising peaks, I could see where the airplane had it all ways over the covered wagon. The air was not without its drawbacks, though. There were plenty of air pockets around, to keep up the interest and ensure nobody fell asleep.

It was hot and stuffy in the cabin. Lorrimer had long since relapsed into the moody silence of a man who prefers the ground. The pilot was Bill Gray, a leathered fifty year old, and an expert. He spent a lot of his working time freighting and was glad of a chance to carry people for a change. He was also very curious to know what it was all about, and maintained a ceaseless barrage of questions, near questions and hints.

At eleven o'clock he turned the little plane a few degrees west.

'Off the straight Vegas course now,' he told me. 'This Lakecrest ought to show up in a few minutes.'

I nodded and nudged Lorrimer to keep out a watch for our destination. Eight minutes later a small town appeared suddenly on the horizon.

'Should be it,' observed Gray. 'No radio here of course so we'll try to identify.'

It wasn't hard. Just outside the town was the airstrip, and here picked out in large white-painted stones, was the legend LAKECREST. As we circled to descend, we could see curious faces upturned on the streets, hands shading eyes which sought to identify us.

Gray braked in the shadow from a small building which was presumably built in anticipation of the day when Lakecrest boasted its own proper airport. A dusty sedan shot round the corner and pulled up. From it stepped a young man in his early twenties with dark unruly hair and a welcoming smile.

'I'm Bert Jobson of the *Bugle*,' he said,

holding out his hand, 'Mr. Franklyn sent me. I'm to take you wherever you want, see you back here when you're through.'

Lorrimer looked at me and I remembered that as special deputy, I was officially in charge.

'Jobson,' I shook hands. 'My name is Preston, special deputy from the mayor's office Monkton City. This is Ed Lorrimer, crime reporter of the *Globe*.'

The young man greeted Lorrimer enthusiastically. To do him credit he didn't come out with any of the hundred questions he was obviously dying to ask the big city newsman. I introduced him to Bill Gray and we all got in the car.

'Where can we leave Mr. Gray, Bert?' I asked. 'He isn't concerned in our trip.'

'Make it somewhere I can get some food, will you, son?' interposed Gray.

'Sure, yes. We have a fine restaurant on Main.'

Lorrimer groaned, and I looked at him sharply. If we were going to get co-operation from these people, that wasn't the way to set about it.

Within five minutes we turned into the inevitable Main Street and dropped off our pilot.

'Think we ought to go and visit your boss first, Bert,' I suggested. 'After he's been to so much trouble.'

He smiled, and it was obvious I'd said the right thing. The offices of the *Lakecrest Bugle* consisted of a double-fronted wooden building two-thirds of the way down Main Street. Along the front, in letters two feet high, was the motto 'The Truth First and Last.'

We all went in, past a couple of sidewalk gapers, and into the editor's office. Josh Franklyn was in his forties, a well-fed brisk-looking man with searching eyes.

'Mr. Franklyn,' I greeted.

He got up from his chair, and we had introductions all round again.

'Mr. Steiner talked to me this morning,' said Franklyn. 'I naturally told him I would be pleased to co-operate with the authorities of your city. What can I do for you, Mr. Preston?'

'Like to see the file on Ellie Colfax if you have it still. I mean the old case, the one you mentioned to Steiner.'

'Certainly. Bert, do you mind?'

Jobson went out of the room. Franklyn said:

'Course, we don't really keep files like the big papers, you realise. We just keep two copies of each edition as a whole. But when I heard Mr. Steiner was interested I put somebody to work clipping out the cuttings on poor little Ellie. We probably have a file by now.'

We had. Bert Jobson brought in a brand new white folder and handed it to his chief, who thanked him and gave it to me.

'Excuse me,' I said.

I put the folder where Lorrimer and I could read through it at the same time. A rape case wasn't something that happened every day in Lakecrest. There was a lot of space given to it, and as far as I could see photographs of almost everybody in town who'd ever so much as spoken to the girl. Which was almost everybody in town. I studied her picture with interest. Unmistakably the same girl who'd died the week before back in Monkton, only here the face was chubbier, due undoubtedly to puppy fat which had since fined down.

'Poor kid,' I muttered.

Franklyn sighed.

'Yes, it was a terrible business, terrible. In some ways, you know, it was best for Lakecrest they never found the man. A lynching never did a town any good and that's what we'd have had sure if the policed picked him up. She was a nice kid, family well thought of round here. Anybody with a son would have been right proud to have him marry Ellie Colfax in a few years' time.'

'That was before this happened,' I said pointedly, indicating the clippings.

He shrugged.

'Oh sure. That changed things naturally. People are what they are, Mr. Deputy. Not my job to criticise, just report the news.'

He looked at me to see whether I wanted to challenge him on that one. I didn't. Instead

I read on through the various reports, scrutinising the badly-printed photographs with special care. If there was anything or anybody to connect Ellie with the Double Dee jay I couldn't find it. I could see from Lorrimer's face he was in the same boat.

'You seen enough yet?' I asked him.

He nodded glumly.

'Yes, thanks.'

Lorrimer handed the file back to Franklyn.

'Some nice touches in there, Mr. Franklyn. Have to hold on to your boys, or we'll be grabbing them off for the *Globe*.'

The editor was delighted, though he tried not to look it.

'Nice of you to say so, Mr. Lorrimer. Anything else I can do for you, gentlemen?'

'If you could just spare Bert for a few more minutes, Mr. Franklyn,' I smiled, 'I'd like to go meet your chief.'

'Certainly, certainly, a pleasure. Bert'll drive you over, and don't hurry on Bert's account. Anything we can do.'

I thanked him, then:

'By the way, anything I ought to know about the chief here before I see him?'

'Hamilton? No, I don't think so. Rudy's a nice feller. Course it's just a small force, only him, one sergeant and four constables. But he keeps the town in order his own way. This isn't one of those places where the public are scared of their own police officers. We have a very fine force, and it's mostly the chief's doing. I told him you may be coming, so he's half-expecting to see you.'

We shook hands with Franklyn, Lorrimer repeating the promises made over the telephone by Steiner, about getting any big story down to Lakecrest the minute it broke. Then we were driving along with the eager Bert again.

'Think Chief Hamilton will co-operate with us, Bert?' I asked casually.

'Mr. Hamilton?' he nodded with enthusiasm. 'There is one great guy. Do you know there's less crime in Lakecrest, taking the size of the population, than in over ninety per cent of towns in the entire State.'

'Doesn't make much of a crime beat for the *Bugle* reporter,' observed Lorrimer. 'Who handles that end?'

'Me,' grinned Bert. 'But I get by. We have a couple of spots in town which are usually reliable for a Saturday night brawl of some kind. It's good exercise for the brain too, trying to make a couple of drunk assaults sound like a crime wave.'

Lorrimer nodded encouragement. Bert stopped outside a white-painted building, two storeys high.

'This is it,' he announced. 'You want me to come inside?'

We told him no thanks and went in. A burly middle-aged man in faded khaki shirt and slacks looked up from a plain wood table which served as a desk.

'You'll be the fellers from Monkton City?' he queried.

'That's right,' I replied. 'Like to see the chief if he's got a minute.'

Before he could reply a door behind him opened, and a tall slim man with wide shoulders stood looking at us. He wore khaki too, but his was pressed and new-looking.

'I'm Chief Hamilton,' he said, in a well-modulated voice. 'C'm on in.'

The chief's private office was sparsely furnished, a few wooden chairs and a battered-looking bookcase filled with well-thumbed volumes. It seemed to be our day for shaking hands with everybody. When we were sitting down I took a better look at our host. He had a sunburnt face, brown skin pulled tight across prominent cheek-bones and a straight nose that was almost pointed. If he'd lived closer to where I did he'd have been able to make a steady living as the proud Indian chief in T.V. westerns. He was talking to me.

'Tell me, what is a special deputy exactly?'

I explained to him about the special powers held by the mayor's office under the city constitution. He listened carefully, then:

'Uh huh. And what's so special that needs a special deputy now? And what makes him you?'

This was the part where I'd have to tread

softly if I was going to spin this man a yarn. Honesty, or a reasonable facsimile thereof, would appear to be the best policy. I mentioned the Ellie Colfax death.

'I read it all very carefully,' he assured us. 'Naturally I was interested. What happened to Ellie those years back is the only major crime committed in this area where I haven't nailed the felon. You don't forget a thing like that.'

'Then you'll recall that someone saw a man leaving the apartment where the Colfax girl was staying?'

'Of course. It was interesting for the first twenty-four hours. Until the police were able to establish that there was no possibility of foul play. In any case the girl was seen alive some hours after this man visited her apartment. What about him?'

'We think we have a lead to the man,' I said carefully.

'So?' He whistled tunelessly. 'It doesn't seem to mean much even if you're right, does it? What does your police department think about it?'

I crossed my fingers mentally, and let go the main lie.

'Remember, we don't have a positive identification. Just the same, it's good enough for the mayor to send me all the way over here to see you. It involves something much bigger, a large business concern in Monkton City. The mayor didn't want to draw any attention to

148

police activity without being absolutely certain he had something solid to walk on. So he's keeping this absolutely to himself until I report back.'

'To himself,' repeated Hamilton. 'Nobody knows anything about it. Just the mayor and you. And the crime reporter of an influential newspaper. Plus the editor, or Lorrimer wouldn't be here. How about the readers, are they in on it too?'

I wished I had that something solid to walk on myself.

'The *Globe* can be trusted on this,' I said in a firm voice. 'His honour hadn't a choice in any case. It was to the *Globe* that this witness took the story. Most papers would have given it a good splashing of ink before they remembered the bit about civic duty. The *Globe* went straight to the mayor, direct.'

Now my unimpressive hand was face up on the table, and in the strong sunlight it didn't give me a lot of faith. Hamilton sat where the dealer sits, thinking it over. Lorrimer squirmed in his chair and was surprised by a quick glare from me. Hamilton noticed the glare, but said nothing. Instead he maintained a rhythmic chewing movement with his jaws and went on thinking.

'I heard of a chief once,' he suddenly said. 'Small town, just like this. Couple of guys arrived to see him. They were big-town lawyers it seemed, wanted access to some file information about an unsolved killing that happened some time back. They were writing a law book on big murder mysteries of modern times. Going to be an important book, this. Naturally the chief would get a good play in their report on this particular case. The chief was tickled, and what harm could it do? The two lawyers thanked him. The case was where a young teenage kid had been beaten to death outside a roadhouse. The police reports seemed to point to a certain man, but there was not enough evidence even for a preliminary hearing, leave alone a trial. So the lawyers made notes, shook hands with the chief, and drove off in this limousine. Only they didn't go back to the big city to write the book. Instead they went out to where he lived, the guy the police thought could have done it. Man was having dinner with his wife and kids. They kicked him to death, right there in the kitchen, in front of a ten year old boy and a girl of six. It turned out the big lawyers were big liars. They were the kid's brothers, the one who got murdered. You know something else? The man didn't do it. The real killer confessed two years later when he was caught doing the same thing again. This chief I was telling you about, he blew his brains out.'

He stopped talking and looked at us quizzically. It was Lorrimer who answered by holding up a foot so Hamilton could see the soft woollen slipper.

'Bunions,' he said sadly. 'I couldn't even kick a mouse without roaring in agony.'

The ghost of a smile played across the lawman's features. He waited for me to say something.

'Chief Hamilton, I'm going to have to ask for your word that you will keep this talk confidential. I'm sticking my neck way, way out by telling you more. There are other necks involved, particularly the one belonging to the mayor of my town.'

I watched him expectantly. He said laconically:

'I'm a police officer. Confidential is just a word. If you're going to give me any information about somebody breaking the law, I'm going to pass it on. No question about that. If you're only talking theories, I'm still a police officer. More than my badge is worth to go off repeating any of the half-grown notions I get told every day.'

In his way he was telling me to go ahead. I dived in.

'You used to have a man on your local radio station here. Big star now, Donny Jingle. Last night his associate, Dave Chisum, was killed in mistake for Jingle. Chisum worked around the local network too, in Jingle's time. We have a witness who says Chisum was the man who visited Ellie Colfax the day she died. I'm not suggesting there was anything wrong about Ellie Colfax's death. The police department where I come from has a reputation for thoroughness. But just the same she died. A week later Chisum died. They both had connections with Lakecrest. Jingle is waiting to be murdered any minute. He has connections with Lakecrest, too. So maybe it's no more than coincidence, probably isn't. But if there is something here in Lakecrest which connects those three people with each other, I want to know what it is. It may even help us to prevent Jingle's murder.'

He listened. Then when I was finished he kept on chewing. Finally he said:

'Donny Jingle? The Double Dee Jay Show? Say that's one I never miss. Sure, I remember him well, and the other man, Chisum. Big surprise to me when Jingle went over there and got so famous and everything. Around here he wasn't much. Used to do this request record programme, Chuck's Choice. Called himself Chuck, those days. Chuck Matthews.'

'Really?' asked Lorrimer. 'You mean that's his real name, chief?'

'Search me. Some of these people use so many different names for business, I often wonder whether they can be certain which is their own. The other one was the same though, Chisum. This is a fact you're telling me, somebody's trying to kill him? I mean Jingle, or Matthews if you like.'

'We'll stick to Jingle if you've no objection,' I replied. 'It's the only name we know him by.

Yes, it's on the level. In fact, there's no doubt Chisum was killed by mistake last night. It was Jingle's car he was trying to start when it blew up.'

He tut-tutted with his tongue, almost wistfully.

'Long way from Lakecrest,' he sighed. 'Suicides, bomb assassinations. Last year we had a widow try to slash her wrists, but she did it about one minute before a neighbour was due to call. Sort of devalued the effort, if you know what I mean. She didn't cut very deep either. Couldn't bear the pain, she said later. Still, I mustn't get off the point. Why are you telling me all this?'

'Wonder if you can think of any connection between Ellie Colfax and Jingle or Chisum. Or both. Maybe the kid was stagestruck or wanted to be a singer or something. You know, maybe haunted the radio station for a chance.'

'Ellie?' He shook his head. 'Not that one. All she thought about was school and church and her family, A real nice kid. That was what made it all the worse. One or two of 'em round here, Ellie's age, they ask for trouble all the time. Swinging their hips around the streets, wearing clothes too old for 'em. Hanging around late diners, and a place outside of town where the truckies stop over. Just looking out for something bad to happen. Trying to make it happen. It would never surprise me what happened to any of that kind. But Ellie. She

153

was real nice.'

'How're the family taking it?' I queried.

His lip curled slightly.

'Taking it? What do you mean, how're they taking it? They spent nineteen years of their lives making that fine girl. Now she's dead. They're taking it hard, Mr. Deputy. Very hard indeed. Joe Colfax is like a bear with its leg caught in a trap. As for Alice, the mother, nobody's even seen her since it happened.'

It was stuffy in the room. I ran a finger round the inside of my collar.

'Did you ever come in contact with Jingle or Chisum while they were working here?'

'Couple of times,' he nodded. 'Didn't like 'em, either one. Though Chuck was the worst, I always suspected. They weren't here all the time, you know. Just did these two programmes here every week, stopped over while they did them. Other days they'd be working on other programmes, other towns.'

'Sure. What didn't you like about them,' I persisted.

He smiled. One of his front lower teeth was broken.

'This is a quiet town we have here. We like it that way. Like quiet people, quiet goings-on. You know? We're not so suspicious of the man from the big city as we were forty years ago. Then we'd likely have run him out just for sneezing. We've made progress. We give him a chance to show his hand. Might even treat him like an ordinary man if he shows the right cards. But people like Jingle and Chisum, we haven't got as far as them yet. You know, the sharp clothes and the big talk, and throwing money around. Foul language came a little too easy to those two, especially Jingle. He had a kind of disrespectful way of talking to a woman, too. That didn't make him anybody's favourite in these parts. The other one, Chisum, he was the brake. Always slowing up the loud-mouth just when it looked as if somebody might haul off and let him have five dollars worth.'

'Five dollars worth?' I queried.

He chuckled briefly.

'That's right. I was forgetting you're a big city man yourself. You sit there so nice and quiet, and you listen so good, I was forgetting you're not a native. Old Judge Miles has a regular scale of charges, like a dentist. Fist-fighting, fair and square, that's a two-dollar fine for a first appearance. Repeat performances are five dollars a ticket. That's what I was meaning.'

'Sounds reasonable. So Jingle and Chisum never had to pay?'

'Nuh. Never would have been any surprise to me though. That man Jingle was never particular about what he said or who heard him.'

I asked him more questions. Was there anybody in particular who disliked either of them. Had he heard of them making any trouble in the neighbouring towns. Had either of them ever been back to Lakecrest since they made good in Monkton City. No, no, no, he told me. I got an impression from the Lakecrest chief that anybody who wanted to blow up jingle ought to get a civic reception, but beyond that no new information. We shook hands all round again and Lorrimer and I went back to the car.

'You don't mind if I say something?' suggested Lorrimer.

'No, what?'

'Oh, nothing particular. Just wanted to hear myself talk. For a while in there, I got a nasty feeling I might be forgetting how it's done,' he grumbled.

'Cheer up, Ed,' I told him. 'Don't forget I'm the big special deputy of this outfit. Nobody said anything about you needing to do any talking. You're just a nosey newspaper guy who came for the ride. Anyway, you're hearing everything that goes on. What more do you want?'

Bert was sucking at a coke bottle, the dewdrops of ice just melting on the outside. Lorrimer groaned.

'Man, that looks like heaven-juice.'

Bert grinned and dived under the seat.

'The St. Peter soft drink company at your service,' he announced proudly.

He handed over a bottle for each of us. I

didn't open mine right away, getting the value of the cold contents by holding the bottle against my forehead. Beside me the newsman gurgled noisily.

'How'd you find the chief?' asked Bert.

'Helpful,' I told him. 'Co-operative.'

'Sure. He's a big asset to a town like this. Good thing for us he's never decided to go for a big city job. They'd snap him up, just like that.'

Bert snapped his fingers.

'Point is, what do we do next, Ed?' I asked him.

He pulled the coke bottle from his mouth reluctantly.

'Why ask me?' he complained. 'I'm just the guy who sits next to you. The one who appears in the magazine pics, Mr. Preston and friend. I don't have any identity at all.'

'On you that Orphan Annie suit looks ridiculous,' I told him. 'What are you beefing about? All right, never mind. Just suppose the great Preston wasn't around, you had to make some great decision all by your under-privileged self. What would you do?'

'You mean apart from head straight to the airstrip?'

'I mean apart from that,' I confirmed.

'Well, you may laugh, but I'd sort of meander over and see the sorrowing parents. What would you do?'

I grinned.

157

'See what being around me has done for your thinking? That's exactly what I'd do. That's what we're going to do.'

The representative from the *Lakecrest Bugle* had been grinning at the routine from the back seat.

'That's the next stop huh? The Colfax place.'

'You know the way, Bert?'

'I ought to,' he replied. 'Beat a path out there about every ten minutes for two solid days last week. You know, when Ellie—'

'Sure. You know the family then, huh? What about them?'

He scratched his head.

'Well I wouldn't say I know them. Kept themselves to themselves since Ellie had that trouble way back. I hadn't started working at the time, so I can't really say I knew them when they were—you know—still circulating.'

Lorrimer grunted.

'They took it pretty hard when the daughter killed herself I imagine?'

'Terrible.' Bert's face was sombre. 'That was a terrible thing to have happened, Mr. Lorrimer. The mother, Alice Colfax, she hasn't even opened the door to anybody since. Joe has to do all the talking for both.'

'We're probably wasting our time, Preston,' growled Lorrimer.

'Probably,' I assented. 'Still, we've come this far, won't hurt to take a ride over. Right,

Bert?'

He pressed the starter.

'Right, Mr. Deputy. Whatever you say.'

In his enthusiasm he started the car with a jerk. Lorrimer stubbed his foot against the front seat. It was the one with the bunions.

To the best of my recollection, Lorrimer kept up the bad language clear out to the Colfax place without once repeating himself.

CHAPTER ELEVEN

The house where Ellie Colfax had lived was a ten-minute ride from the town centre. It lay at the end of a dirt road which looked as if it could be murder in the winter. It was a two-storey frame building painted green and white. It looked like the picture of home on the Christmas cards. There was even a green and white picket fence, and everything looked to be in good condition. Joe Colfax was evidently a man who took proper care of his home, if the outside was anything to judge by, and it usually is.

A man sat on the porch. He'd been reading a newspaper, but as he saw the car approaching he lowered the paper and watched our approach intently. Lorrimer and I got out and opened the gate. As we walked up the path the man got up, opened the door and shouted into the house.

'Stay where you are, Alice. People coming.'

Then he turned to wait for us.

Joe Colfax was approaching fifty, and the years had not treated him well. His hair was straggly grey, and the once-round face had sagged into fleshy folds. The eyes which now studied us warily had grown weary of such encounters. They were tired, and the marks of pain were there. He wore a grubby check shirt and crumpled pants. The beard on his face had been growing for three or four days.

I spoke first.

'Mr. Colfax?'

He nodded, but did not speak.

'My name is Preston. I'm a special—'

'I know who you are,' he snapped. 'And your newspaper pal too. What do you want?'

That caught me in mid-stride. If he knew who we were, somebody must have told him, and since we hadn't mentioned our visit to anybody I was trying to guess who it might have been.

'Mr. Colfax, I'd like you to know we have no wish to intrude on your grief. If it wasn't absolutely necessary we wouldn't be here.'

He sneered.

'You can stow all that talk. I've heard the sob-sister stuff from too many in the past week. All for a few rotten lines in some smear newspaper. One dame actually wanted to get a picture of my wife holding all Ellie's baby

160

clothes. I tried to hit her, but somebody stopped me.'

Lorrimer clucked sympathetically.

'Mr. Colfax, we haven't come in connection with your daughter's death. Not specifically.'

Colfax inspected him like something he'd just noticed crawling out of the woodwork.

'Really. Just what did you come for? Specifically.'

He was standing with his hands on his hips, feet apart, in front of the door of his house. He made me think of a man who'd reached the last ditch and was now getting ready to fight for his life. Considering the double tragedy he'd had to suffer over his daughter it wasn't hard to visualise how he felt.

'Do you think we could sit down for a minute?' I asked.

'Out here, if you must,' he agreed grudgingly.

We arranged ourselves on an assortment of wooden chairs, all painted in cheerful colours.

'You say you know who we are,' I began. 'Don't you know why we're here as well?'

'Wouldn't ask if I knew.'

'Very well. There's been an attempt made to murder a man in our town. That's Monkton City. The attempt failed, but another man died instead, so we're already talking about murder. The point is, the killer is certain to have another try at the man he failed to kill the first time.'

161

'What's that got to do with me?' he asked suspiciously.

'Probably nothing at all,' I admitted. 'But we can't afford to ignore anything, no matter how small, which might put us on the trail of this murderer. A man's life is at stake.'

I let him think about it for a minute or two. There was probably nothing of value Joe Colfax could tell us. However, I wanted to be quite sure of that before we left. If we annoyed him now, and he threw us out, we could just miss some small detail. My business was not to annoy him. It was Lorrimer who spoke next. I'd no idea his voice could be so gentle.

'The man who died by mistake, Mr. Colfax, he left a widow and two little kids. He was murdered by mistake, but that doesn't leave those kids any better off. We have to find the man who did this. You've lost somebody, you know how that widow is feeling today. Will you help us?'

It made an impression. Some of the surly expression left Colfax's face when Lorrimer mentioned his loss.

'Two kids, you say? That's awful.'

I looked at Lorrimer. He had the ball.

'It's awful,' he agreed. 'It could get worse, there might be others.'

The bereaved man nodded.

'O.K. If I can help.'

I told him roughly what had happened. I didn't mention any names.

'You probably know the case I'm talking about now,' I finished. 'It's had enough publicity.'

He shook his head.

'Nope. I don't know anything about it. Haven't opened a newspaper or turned on the television since—since last week. I'm just not interested in what's happening in the rest of the world.'

Now I was coming to the hard part.

'The man who died was named Chisum, Dave Chisum.' I was watching his face to see if the name produced any reaction. Nothing. 'On the afternoon of the day your daughter died, Chisum went to visit her.'

Now there was reaction. His eyes came suddenly to life.

'You mean you think this Chisum could have murdered my girl, killed her?'

There was eagerness in his voice, eagerness to be told that somebody else had taken Ellie away from him. Someone who could be hated and reviled. An outlet for the bottled-up emotion which was now only black despair. I shook my head.

'I think that's out of the question. Ellie was seen by a number of reliable, impartial witnesses, hours after the man's visit. But it does establish a connection between them. We want to know what that was. Did she ever mention the name Chisum to you?'

The hope was gone and he was glum again.

'No. Never heard of him.'

'He used to work around here. On the local radio station. He and another man, named Chuck Matthews.'

For a moment I thought I detected a change in his face, but it was quickly gone.

'Sorry, I can't help you. Never heard of either one of 'em.'

Up till then he'd been co-operating. Grudgingly, but nevertheless co-operating. Now he'd put up a stone wall. He was patiently waiting for us to leave. I nodded at Lorrimer and we stood up.

'Well thanks for listening to us, Mr. Colfax.'

'It's all right. Hope you catch this guy. Sorry I wasn't able to help.'

Lorrimer held out his hand.

'Thanks for trying anyway. By the way, when will Mrs. Colfax be coming back?'

He shot it out suddenly. Colfax took a step, his face like granite.

'Coming back? I don't understand you. She's in the house, pretty sick. Now you get outa here.'

'No, she isn't,' contradicted Lorrimer. 'She's gone off somewhere, and I don't believe you know where. You're just bluffing. There's nobody in that house.'

'There is, there is,' insisted Colfax, but he was cowering as though to shield himself from a blow. 'She's in bed, hasn't been up in a week. She's a very sick woman.'

164

'What does the doctor say about her? What did he prescribe?' pressed Lorrimer.

'That's none of your business. This is a family matter.'

'No, it isn't. It's a matter for the police. Woman disappears under mysterious circumstances, husband doesn't know where she is. Or says he doesn't,' continued Lorrimer relentlessly. 'If we went to Chief Hamilton with this he'd have a dozen men out here in no time. You know what they'd be looking for, Mr. Colfax? A fresh-dug grave.'

'No. No.'

Colfax sank down in a chair, face buried in his hands. His tubby body heaved as the sobs rocked him. When he looked up again there were tears coursing through the stubble on his cheeks.

I exchanged uncomfortable glances with Lorrimer. 'Mr. Colfax,' I said, keeping my voice soft, 'You'd better tell us about it. It has to come out in the end.'

He nodded, took his hands away from his face.

'Come in the house.'

We followed through the flimsy wood door. Inside, the place was untidy. It looked as if somebody had not been bothering to clean up for several days. The special kind of untidiness a man falls into when there's no woman around. Colfax sat in a wicker chair, blowing his nose violently on a coloured handkerchief.

165

'You're right,' he told me. 'It has to come out. Might as well be now. I been near sick with worry. Maybe, if I talk to you fellers, I'll sleep tonight.'

Just take it easy, Mr. Colfax. Tell us in your own way.'

Lorrimer had shed the rough tone he'd used before. Colfax didn't seem to notice.

'You ever see my wife in her younger days? Guess you wouldn't have,' he sighed.

We both shook our heads.

'Prettiest thing in town. Ask anybody. You call these dames on the movies pretty, you should have seen my Alice.'

He paused to see if we'd interrupt. We didn't.

'I was a lot older of course. Sixteen years. I had this house and a good car, pretty well fixed in my job. I was thirty-three years old, Alice was seventeen.' He chuckled. 'I tell you, there were a few surprised faces around Lake-crest when she up and married me. Heads were shaken, too. I was a bit set in my ways, how could I keep a rein on a high-spirited gal like Alice, they said. Well, they were wrong. She settled down to make me a wife a man could be proud of. Then Ellie came along, and I guess I had about everything in the world a man could want.'

He sighed and looked at the thick black hair on the backs of his hands. For a moment there was silence. I was afraid he was going to break

166

down again. Instead he went on with the story.

'Things were fine for years. The money was coming in pretty good from my invention, and we were all set. Then,' his face clouded over, 'Then there was this thing with Ellie. Just like somebody switched off the sun. That was a real bad time. Ellie had to have quiet and rest. The doc said it was a miracle she didn't go out of her mind. But it was Alice suffered the most. She blamed herself for the whole thing, said she should never have let Ellie out of her sight. She started moping around. The place got neglected, she couldn't even bother fixing her hair any more. She—she started to get feeble-minded. Doc said he'd seen it before. There was nothing he could do for her. She'd either pull out of it when she was ready, or else she'd just get worse. You know something funny?'

He didn't mean funny, he meant ironic. Joe Colfax didn't know the word ironic, but he knew better than most people what it meant.

'It was Ellie who stopped her mother going insane. She waited on her, nursed her, never complained once. All those years. Alice began to get better, started cleaning up the place again, looking after herself.'

'When was this, Mr. Colfax?' interposed Lorrimer. 'The improvement?'

'Not long back. Two, three months. The doc said it was a miracle, or near one. For a few weeks it really began to look as if everything

167

was going to be all right again. Then last week, Ellie suddenly left home. Didn't say a word to me. Just up and quit. Next thing we knew was when Chief Hamilton knocked on the door and told us she'd—told us what had happened.'

He was quiet again. A bee droned noisily against the curtained window. The white wooden clock ticked insistently away from its place on the wall. Photographs of friends and relatives stared inquisitively down at Joe Colfax, a beaten figure huddled in a wicker chair.

'I had to go and see Ellie. Had to go and identify her so they'd be sure she was my baby. I couldn't let Alice face it, so I went alone. When I got back she was gone. Since then there's been no word. Nothing.'

He looked up to let us know the story was finished. Lorrimer cleared his throat.

'You've done nothing about finding her, at all?'

Colfax heaved his shoulders.

'I've telephoned every relative she ever had. None round here, you understand. Alice's folks came here from Arizona in the first place. Now they're gone, there is nobody in this neighbourhood.'

'But supposing she's come to some harm?' insisted the man from the *Globe*. 'What's to say she went off of her own free will? She could have been kidnapped or something.'

168

Puzzlement showed on Colfax's face.

'Why would she leave a note like that if she was kidnapped?'

'Note? What note? You didn't mention any note.'

'Oh. Well, I should have. She left me this note saying she couldn't stand it here without Ellie and she was going off for a few days to put things right.'

It was Lorrimer's turn to look puzzled.

'Put things right? What things?'

'I don't know exactly. I imagined she just meant to put herself right, you know. What are you gentlemen going to do about Alice?'

I thought it was time I said something.

'I don't know there's much we can do, Mr. Colfax. The lady is over twenty-one, she has a right to move about in this country if she wants to. You're satisfied that she knew what she was doing when she left the house. I appreciate your personal position. You're worried and you miss your wife. That's natural. But it isn't a police matter. Not yet.'

He nodded unhappily.

' 'Bout sums it up. It doesn't really matter to anybody else but me.'

'She's had a nasty shock, Mr. Colfax. The last one was bad enough. This one is worse. For the moment I should assume she's gone off for a few days' rest, maybe even to the coast. If she doesn't come back after say another three days, get in touch with Chief

169

Hamilton. Tell him the story. He's a good man, he'll know what to do.'

'Hamilton? He's a fine man,' agreed Colfax. 'Why he even phoned to tell me you fellers would probably call here to see me. Give Alice a chance to pretty herself up, he said, if she'd a mind to meet you.'

'Very considerate of him,' contributed Lorrimer flatly.

I got up and said:

'We'd better be on our way. Just one thing I'd like to ask before we go. And remember, you may be the means of preventing a murder, Mr. Colfax. Are you sure you don't remember the name of Chuck Matthews?'

If there'd been a flicker of recognition the first time the name was mentioned, there was no sign of it on Colfax's face now.

'No. Sorry.'

We said goodbye, and left him sitting there. As we clicked the wooden gate shut Lorrimer said:

'What d'you think?'

'I think the guy has a pack of trouble,' I replied. 'Maybe there's more to come. Like to find Alice, see what she's up to.'

'Like what things is she putting right for example.'

'Like that, for example.'

The irrepressible Bert was dozing in the car.

'You had a good long interview,' he remarked. 'Better than I ever managed to get.'

170

'Don't worry about it, Bert,' soothed Lorrimer. 'We didn't get anything we hadn't already seen in the *Bugle.*'

'Zasso? Well, there you are,' he beamed. 'Finest paper of its size in the whole state. Where to now?'

'We'll just call in and thank your boss for everything, then we'll be off home,' I replied.

Ten minutes later we were outside the office of the finest paper of its size in the whole state. I asked Bert to search around and find our pilot, Bill Gray. Then Lorrimer and I went into the editor's room.

He asked how we'd made out and we gave him a rough idea of what we'd been doing. We carefully forgot to tell him Alice Colfax was missing.

'By the way, saw a picture of Mrs. Colfax up at the house,' I told him. 'I have a strong impression her face is familiar to me.'

'Could be,' he mused. 'She got a lot of publicity at the time of Ellie's—er—case.'

'No,' I wasn't convinced. 'I didn't mean in connection with the case. Tell you the truth, I'm not sure what I do mean. But I'll lay awake tonight if I don't try to pin it down. You must have quite a few pictures of Mrs. Colfax on file. Would you mind if I borrowed a couple?'

He looked at me shrewdly, finally nodded his head.

'Sure, certainly.'

Going to the door he spoke to a girl who sat

at a desk typing furiously. Then he came back to me.

'Know how you feel, Mr. Preston. Thing like that can drive a man to drink. It's by chasing these mental butterflies you sometimes land a major story. You might have made a good newspaperman.'

'Or detective,' put in Lorrimer snidely.

Franklyn chuckled with embarrassment.

'Oh say, that's right. I was almost forgetting.'

He was saved by the little tubby girl who flounced in, handed him a thick envelope, and flounced out again importantly.

'Had to let her do the movie reviews this week,' explained Franklyn. 'Regular man is sick. Now she thinks she's Lunella Parsons.'

He untied the green ribbon round the envelope and took out a handful of glossy pictures.

'These are all the shots we used on the first story about Ellie.' Lowering his voice he said confidentially, 'Just between ourselves, Alice being a local woman and everything, I didn't think it would be any kindness to print a more recent picture of her when this tragedy happened last week. I used one or two of these again, although they're four years old.'

While he was talking he was sorting through the prints, picking out those of Alice Colfax and passing them to me. There were seven altogether.

I found myself looking at a handsome woman, whom I knew was in her early thirties at the time the pictures were taken. Alice Colfax had soft honey-blonde hair, with the same wide-set eyes and pronounced cheekbones as her daughter. Ellie had been pretty, but country-pretty. Alice was a striking-looking woman who'd draw attention in places bigger than Lakecrest. Joe Colfax had not been exaggerating. I selected two of the prints. Franklyn said:

'Does it come to mind?'

'Not yet,' I admitted. 'But if you don't mind me borrowing these for a day or two, I'll stare at them till something clicks.'

'Good for you. Sure, you take them and welcome,' grinned the editor. 'Anything else I can do for you gentlemen? After all, you came a long way. Hope it was worth it.'

'I think it will be, in the end,' I assured him. 'In any case, nobody could have been to more trouble than you, Mr. Franklyn. I want you to know how much I appreciate it. Ready?'

I asked Lorrimer the last part. He winked.

'You go ahead, Preston. Just want to thank Mr. Franklyn here, and arrange the details for passing down the story when it breaks.'

'Sure.'

I went out to the car. Bill Gray was lying full-length on the back seat.

'Ah,' he greeted. 'The special envoy. Let me tell you, friend, you missed the finest steak in

173

the northern hemisphere.'

'At least you didn't,' I complained. 'Did you eat so much you can't even sit straight?'

With many grunts and sighs he pulled himself upright.

'Flying is an exacting profession,' he lectured. 'A wise aviator takes care of his body at all times.'

'Huh.'

Lorrimer came out, and sat in front next to Bert.

'O.K., Bert. Last haul,' I announced. 'Back to the airstrip.'

We moved away from the kerb. Lorrimer leaned over the seat to whisper to me.

'That bit about Colfax's invention,' he uttered hoarsely. 'Guess what he invented?'

'No bid,' I replied.

'A detonator. The Colfax detonator.'

And that gave us both something to think about on the bumpy ride home.

CHAPTER TWELVE

Lorrimer and I parked at Monkton City airport. He felt he had to get straight back to the *Globe* to make his report to Shad Steiner. I felt I had to get a shower and something to eat before starting anything new. One thing about this business had already registered firmly.

Every contact and every situation seemed to lead direct to another. No provision seemed to be made for incidental matters like sleeping and eating, a couple of habits I'd picked up in early life and didn't seem able to shake. If I went to Steiner now I knew I'd be off again on some other smell, and so forth. There were no natural breaks in the programme. As the thought crossed my mind I felt myself grinning. I was even starting to think in television terms.

At the Parkside Towers I closed the door of my apartment with a feeling of relief. Everybody has to have somewhere to go, a burrow where the outside can be shut out for a while. A place to think private thoughts, repair the latest damage to the ego, check over the stock-pile of winter nuts. In the cool of the apartment I realised how tired I was. After all I'd had little enough sleep the night before, and the morning had not exactly been restful. I looked at the bed with longing as I stripped off, dropping my clothes in all directions. It wouldn't have taken much persuasion to get me stretched out on that inviting softness. Instead I dragged my unco-operative feet to the shower cabinet. Starting the water off lukewarm, I had a good soak for a couple of minutes before adjusting the mix-control to full cold. The icy needles pierced into my skin, even penetrated the fog around my head, dispersing it gradually until I began telling myself I was quite fresh again. When my teeth started chattering I hopped out, wrapped a towelling robe around me and went back into the living-room. My timing was picking up, too. As I stepped through the door the telephone yammered.

'Yup.'

It was Florence Digby's voice. A distant, dignified Digby.

'Oh, Mr. Preston, I've found you at last.'

'Look, Miss Digby, I've been out of town. I tried to call you at the office before I left this morning, but you hadn't arrived.'

Brief pause while she assimilated that one.

'I see. Practically everyone in town has been trying to reach you. Sergeant Randall called just after lunch, he sounded bad-tempered. A Mr. Jingle—would that be any relation to Donny Jingle the television man?'

'An identical twin,' I told her. 'Anybody else?'

'A Miss Blane called three times. She seemed very worried about not finding you. I have her number here.'

That was Florence's way of finding out whether I already knew Miss Blane. Also whether Miss Blane came under the file reference of Investigations or Personal Business. I wasn't going to satisfy her curiosity.

'Let me have the number please, I'll call the lady.'

I wrote it down as Miss Digby read it out.

176

'Got it.'

'There was another lady too,' the inflexion on the word lady could be interpreted any way I chose. 'A Miss Nicola Hardin. Said would you please call her at her office at the first opportunity.'

'Will do. That the lot?'

'One more. A man whose name I didn't quite catch. He sounded terribly worried about something. He called twice. I asked if you could call back, but he said he didn't know quite where he could be located. Said he had to keep moving around and you'd understand.'

Ah.

'Now think, Miss Digby. Was the name Shoeman? Mo Shoeman?'

She thought about it.

'It could have been. Yes I think it might have been. Sorry not to be positive, but he was in such a hurry both times, talking in this hoarse whisper.'

'That's all right. Thanks for letting me know. I won't be coming in this afternoon. If you want me I'll probably be reached at the A.I.C.T. building.'

'Very well.'

After I put the phone down, I realised the water on my body was beginning to chill me. I towelled vigorously and felt better. Very much better. As I rubbed away I was thinking about the people who'd been trying to contact me. Thinking especially about two of them. An ad-man named Mo Shoeman who was suspected by the police of killing a man by mistake, thinking he was a television d-j named Donny Jingle. And a singer named Whitney Blane who had good reason to hate the same Donny Jingle, and who, it seemed, had a brother named Mo Shoeman. I wanted to talk to Mo, but knew I'd have to wait until he chose to contact me again. His sister was less of a problem. I had her telephone number right in front of me. I lit an Old Favourite and dialled the number. The girl must have been sitting on top of the instrument at the other end. I heard only one short brrr before the receiver was lifted. A girl's voice, low and guarded:

'Hallo.'

'Miss Blane, this is Mark Preston. You've been trying to get in touch with me.'

'Oh.'

She didn't sound wild with enthusiasm. I waited.

'It wasn't anything important, Mr. Preston. Just wanted to—to apologise for the way I acted last night. Guess I was pretty drunk.'

She'd been too long remembering what it was she wanted me for. I said:

'No need to apologise. Nobody got hurt. Still, I appreciate it. Maybe we could start over next time we meet."

'Fine,' she said eagerly. Too eagerly.

We passed a few more civil comments in the same vein, then hung up. I cursed softly. What

I really needed was food. What I was going to get was a fast ride round to Whitney Blane's apartment.

I tossed on some fresh linen and a lightweight suit. Ten minutes later I was getting hard glances from other people who wanted the use of the road that hot Friday afternoon. At three thirty I was putting weight on the buzzer at Number 63, Bellevue Apartments.

It was several minutes before anybody answered. The door opened a few inches and I was looking into the startled face of Whitney Blane.

'Oh. It's you.'

'It is,' I admitted. 'Can I come in?'

'Not now. I'm sorry. I'm pretty busy. Call me later.' She tried to shut the door but something got in the way. We both looked down. It was my foot.

'Better let me in, honey. I can probably help.'

Without waiting for her to give me an argument, I heaved on the door, and she stood back to let me pass. Her face was pale, and looked almost deathly against the rich cherry hair. She wore a bathrobe pulled carelessly around her, but I hadn't come to peep. She didn't seem to care whether I did or not.

In the sunlight the place was even louder in the way of decor. Sun can play the devil with things you might not notice under artificial

179

light. Like the thin film of dust which I could now see on much of the furniture. Or the small clustered wrinkles at the sides of the singer's eyes.

She sat down listlessly.

'All right,' she said wearily, 'You're in. What's it all about?'

I stood listening. When I didn't reply she said:

'You don't talk much, do you?'

'No. I'm a listener. Listen.'

I held a finger to my lips as I walked towards the door leading to the bedroom. Whitney Blane was out of her chair and standing with her back to the door before I could reach it.

'Stand aside like a good girl,' I told her.

She shook her head.

'You clear out before I call the police.'

'This is no time for jokes, Whitney. He's in there and the police would love to know it. You're not calling anybody. Anyhow, I only want to talk to him. Maybe I can help.'

'The best way you can help is to mind your own business,' she hissed.

'Look, I have to talk to Mo,' I said gently. 'Don't make me lift you out of the way. Mo,' I raised my voice, 'tell her it's OK. Tell her to let me in.'

From the bedroom there was no sound.

'That's how much he trusts you,' she sneered.

I sighed, caught her by one arm and twisted her out of the way. At the same moment I stepped quickly to the door, opened it and slipped inside. There was nobody in sight. I knelt down and looked under the black silk divan covering. Nothing. Most of one wall was taken up by a floor-to-ceiling wardrobe. I slid back one of the doors. There was a solid row of evening gowns in front of me.

Whitney leaned in the doorway smiling in mockery.

'The blue and silver should look good on you,' she offered.

Stepping into the room she closed the door. Almost at the same instant I heard the outer door of the apartment click shut. I said a word and crossed to the bedroom door. It was locked. Whitney chuckled and threw a metal object on to the black silk bed. It was a key.

'I haven't got to the stage where I need to lock 'em in the bedroom with me. Help yourself.'

It took five seconds to get the key, another five to open the door. Although I knew I was licked I went through the motions. From the front door I saw the red indicator light on the elevator panel winking at '1'. He was already at street level. I went back into the apartment and looked out a window. On the street below a round man of medium height scuttled across the sidewalk and dived into a yellow sedan. I couldn't read the number. I said that word again and turned back into the room.

She was sitting in one of the fragile white-painted chairs. Her legs were crossed and the bathrobe had fallen away at the join, leaving most of her thighs on view. She didn't seem to notice. I noticed.

'That's twice you said a bad word,' she reproved.

'You ought to hear what I'm thinking,' I assured her. 'Neat trick, that. Where was he? In the bathroom?'

'Where was who, Mr. Preston? Ain't nobody here but us party-goers.'

'About that party last night,' I reminded. 'You clean forgot to mention that the brother who first brought you to this evil old town had a name. Especially you forgot to mention the name was Mo Shoeman.'

'Did I?' she pouted. 'When I'm on the town, Mr. Preston, I don't want to spend all my time talking about a pack of stuffy old relatives.'

'Not so stuffy,' I disagreed. 'After all he should have had a little gossip-value, particularly last night after he killed a man.'

'Mo did that? My, my. I must watch that boy. He'll be going out with girls next thing.'

She was completely self-possessed now. The danger was past, her brother was still free. It was obvious she didn't give the slightest thought to her own involvement. I sat down and stuck a cigarette in my face. She held out a hand, clicking her fingers. I passed over the pack.

'We'd better have a talk, Whit.'

'So talk,' she shrugged. 'It won't change anything.'

'You were trying to get in touch with me this morning. I think I know why. You were worried because you knew Mo was missing and you thought I might either know where he was, or help you find him.'

'That what I thought?'

'It was. Then, some time between your call to me and mine back, Mo turned up. He came here and so you didn't need me any more.'

'I just wanted to tell you I was sorry about last night—' she began.

I interrupted.

'Sorry? You? When was a lush like you ever sorry about anything she did?' I asked her bitingly.

She coloured.

'Listen don't come in here talking to me that way—'

'I'll talk to you any way I please. A dumb dame who'll let her own brother go roaming off into God knows what danger doesn't deserve any sympathy. Has he got a gun?'

Immediately she forgot I'd insulted her.

'Why?'

'Has he got a gun?' I repeated.

'Yes. An old thing he brought back from the war. Why?'

'Great. Half the police in the state are

watching out for him. They think he's dangerous. Suppose they spot him and he gets excited. Goes for the gun. You think they're going to stop to reason with him? They'll smear him all over the street.'

Her lip trembled.

'Don't talk like that.'

'Murder is a rough business. Don't expect every cop in town to bust out crying because he's your brother. All they'll see is a murder suspect pulling a gun on them. They won't ask any questions. They'll cut him down like a mad dog.'

A tear squeezed out from one eye and rolled slowly down the oval face. She tried to keep her voice from trembling but without much success.

'You love it don't you? Love the blood and the killing. We're not people to you. Just suspects and wanted notices.'

I thought she'd been softened up enough.

'No, Whit, you're wrong there. I just want you to see this the way it is. It doesn't have to end like that. Tell me where he is, where I can find him. It might not be too late.'

'It was too late a long time ago,' she said hopelessly. 'Mo has to do what he has to do.'

'He's going to kill Jingle isn't he?' I asked.

She nodded.

'Do you know where he's going to do it?'

'No. He didn't tell me anything about it. Just came to tell me goodbye. He knows he won't get away with killing Donny. But he doesn't care, he's gone past caring.'

'Can you tell me any more about it?' I persisted.

She looked at me with tear-filled eyes.

'I've told a lot of men a lot of lies. You'll be able to believe that without half-trying. But this is true. I don't know any more than what I've told you. Mo got here not more than a few minutes before you telephoned. He was very excited and it took me a long time to calm him down. He hadn't even had a cup of coffee since yesterday. I fixed him some food. He's my brother and I know him, who better? I thought he could eat, then afterwards we'd sit and talk quietly. I'd find out what it was all about. I would have too, only you got here before we were properly started. I tried to get him to trust you, but he said no. He said trusting somebody was one thing, but asking a man with a private licence to let him go, knowing he was going to kill a man, that was different. That was asking a little too much.'

I nodded.

'He was right, too. I couldn't have done that. Still can't let him get away with it.'

I got up. She watched me anxiously.

'What're you going to do?'

I patted her on the shoulder.

'I'm going to stop him, honey. If I can. And try to have him picked up all in one piece.'

'I trust you,' she said in a small girl voice.

'Thanks. If he gets in touch with you, try to talk him out of it, will you?'

She said she would, and I left her there. A worried, frightened girl who was waiting to hear whether her one anchor in an unsavoury world was going to be taken away. Not at all like the big-city dame of the previous night.

To know people you have to see them in trouble.

CHAPTER THIRTEEN

I stopped off at a stand-up diner for a quick sandwich and a glass of milk. The sandwich was packed with vitamins. After I located one crawling over the salad, I settled for the milk. Sorting my loose change I went into the end booth of a row of pay-phones and called Shad Steiner at the *Globe*.

'Shad? Preston. You got enough from Lorrimer, or you want me to drop by?'

'No thanks,' he told me. 'Ed has it covered: Useful little trip eh?'

'We'll know better when we find more of the pieces,' I replied. 'By the way, who does a special deputy have to see? Shouldn't I go to the mayor's office and report, or something?'

'Normally, yes. But I have a message here for you from the office. The mayor is now satisfied with the police investigations into the

186

case. He thanks you for your citizen-like attitude, and asked me to say how much he personally appreciates what you've done. Now the job is being so capably handled by the police department; there will be no need to ask you to make further sacrifices. Let me have the badge back when you can.'

He said all that in a perfectly serious tone: I wished I was able to see his face.

'How do you do it, Shad?'

'Do what?' he queried, trying to sound offended. 'Just a case of a fearless editor with a proper devotion to civic interests.'

'Sure. Did you talk to somebody at A.I.C.T. about me not showing for work this morning?'

'I certainly did. Talked with a girl who is a kind of office manager for the Donny Jingle circus.'

'Nicola Hardin,' I prompted.

'That was the name, yes. She kept me hanging on while she cleared with somebody else, then told me the network understood the position, and you were to get over there as soon as you returned from Lakecrest.'

'You told them it was Lakecrest?'

'Was there any harm in it?' he countered.

'Probably not.'

Just the same I wished he hadn't mentioned exactly where I'd gone.

'Where are you now, Preston?'

'I'm on my way to work. Why?'

'Sergeant Randall of the homicide detail

was in this morning. Had another fellow with him. I didn't know the second man. If he was from our police department, he must be very new. Funny thing, he seemed to be in charge, too.'

'What'd they want?'

Shad chuckled.

'They wanted to know what the idea was, your becoming a special deputy all of a sudden. Seems somebody in the mayor's office must have mentioned it, and word got down to the department. They also knew I had a hand in it somewhere. One of the things they naturally wanted to know more than anything, was where you'd gone.'

'You tell 'em?'

He snorted.

'No, I did not. It was early enough for Randall to have phoned the chief in Lakecrest and come to some kind of understanding with him. That I was not having.'

'Did Randall get sore?' I asked.

'He went a kind of purple colour. Very bad sign on a heavy man like that. I told him it was not strictly any of my business, and that if the department felt they ought to know, they should take it up with the mayor's office.'

'H'm.'

We talked for another minute or two. Steiner was trying to find out which way my thoughts were leading, and I was trying not to tell him. As newspaper men go, Shad Steiner is well up front when it comes to straight dealing, but just the same he's still editor of the *Globe*. The place for stories is in print, and the Double Dee Jay thing came with a side order of nitro-glycerine. If the story was anywhere close to what I imagined I didn't want it blowing up in my face. So I stalled him along, promised to get in touch when anything broke. Then I hung up, and stood trying to make up my mind what came next.

That isn't strictly accurate. I knew what came next. I had to get over to homicide and try to make peace talk with Rourke and Randall. What I was really making up my mind about was how to keep them happy without giving too much away.

The desk sergeant was a grizzled old-timer I'd known for years.

'Ah,' he greeted, with a leer, 'if it isn't Daniel himself.'

'Old age is affecting your memory,' I told him. 'The name is Preston.'

He leaned across the scarred wooden desk-top and smiled.

'There was nobody named Preston in the lion's den, son. The lions are upstairs, and you are Daniel, believe it. I have orders to put you on the air at five o'clock. You only just beat me to it by ten minutes.'

He pointed at the ancient clock on the wall behind him.

'On the air?' I puzzled. 'What did I do?'

'Search me,' he returned. 'Can't be nothing too bad, though. It wasn't to be a 'shoot on sight'. Just bring in for routine questioning.'

'Don't sound so disappointed,' I said acidly. 'O.K. to go up?'

'Help yourself.'

I went up.

A few years before World War I, Monkton City decided it had progressed far enough to justify a police department in place of the sheriff's office. So they built a four-storey horror which was in keeping with the other architecture of the period, and the department was born. That was over a half-century ago. The population has increased five times since those days. The size of the department has only doubled, but even so, there are twice as many people in the building as it was built for originally. We talk a lot about what a progressive community we are, and we can show you the city hall, a couple of library buildings and other evidence of community pride. Other places may have crowded jails, resulting in insanitary and inhumane conditions for the criminals. Not Monkton. We have built three new jails during that half-century, each one being more in step with modern thinking on the punishment of wrong-doers. Naturally, if a city is going to avoid unfavourable publicity over things like that, there isn't going to be a lot left in the city funds for extraneous expense. Like pouring away the taxpayers money to provide the police department with decent working conditions, for instance. So the lawboys stayed where they'd been for fifty years, even with some of the original equipment. The building was badly lit, and ventilated in accordance with the most up-to-date standards of nineteen-o-something. It was dirty and crowded, and a faint smell of mustiness lingered everywhere. The homicide detail rated just three rooms on the third floor of this relic.

I knocked at a door marked 'PRIVATE' and went in. Two men looked up from a report they were reading. One was Randall. The other was a man in his late twenties, a smooth dresser with crew-cut blond hair. I noticed with relief that Rourke was not behind his desk, and that the surface had that tidy look which could mean he was off duty.

Randall grinned with malice.

'Special Deputy Preston, as I live and breathe.'

'Hear you're looking for me?' I questioned.

'Come in and sit down,' he invited.

I lifted an old wooden chair from its place by the wall, parked it in front of the desk, sat down.

'This is Preston,' announced Randall to Crew-Cut.

The blond man looked at me in a way that said he'd remember me.

'We've been anxious to have a talk with you,

Mr. Preston.'

His voice was pleasant, but impersonal.

'Really?'

I pushed an Old Favourite in my mouth, lit it. Then I said:

'I usually like to know who it is I'm talking to.'

'Say, I forgot you wouldn't know. Being out of town on special investigations so much, and all,' Randall replied nastily. 'This is Mr. Brand. Mr. Brand is from the State Capital, Preston. You want to ask any more questions?'

'No. I guess that about covers it.'

'Correct. That covers it just fine. Now you realise there isn't any need to be coy about speaking up in front of Mr. Brand, start talking.'

'What about?' I hedged.

Randall had evidently been having a trying day. He was not in the mood to cat and mouse around with me. 'Let's try this television killing. What about that?'

I shrugged.

'I gave you my statement on that last night. If you're thinking I held out on you, you're mistaken. I told you everything I know.'

Brand waved an admonitory finger.

'You ought to watch those tenses, Mr. Preston. You told the sergeant everything you knew, not everything you know. What was true last night is unlikely to be true this afternoon.'

'That's right,' chimed Randall. 'Plenty

happened since last night. I appreciate your modesty, Preston. Very becoming. But let's not forget the distinction his honour conferred on you this morning. A special deputy yet.'

He tut-tutted. I pulled out my piece of tin.

'You want to see my badge? If the mayor wants me to discuss his office business, I imagine he'll give me clearance on the telephone. Mind if I call him up?'

I reached for the telephone. Randall's huge hand clamped over mine, and he glared.

'Don't let's play footsie, Preston. You've been off the mayor's staff since one p.m. All that badge makes you is a life member of the Lone Ranger club.'

Brand nodded.

'I have talked to the mayor. When I explained the nature of my business he saw immediately that there would be no necessity for his office to make a separate investigation.'

I suddenly felt lonely. Randall smiled unpleasantly.

'Just what is the nature of your business, Mr. Brand?'

He shook his head.

'I'm interested in the murder of this man Chisum last night. That's all I propose to tell you.'

'And the mayor has given us a release on anything you found out while you were working for him,' finished Randall. 'So now will you get on with it?'

I stubbed the smoke in a metal ashtray on Randall's desk.

'Just a one-way trade?' I parried. 'I tell you what I know, and you guys tell me nothing. How'm I supposed to earn a living?'

'You could try honest work,' snorted the sergeant. 'Stop breaking my heart.'

'Mr. Preston, could I remind you of just one thing, since you mention making a living?' put in Brand. 'You operate on a licence which is issued by the city administration. These licences are all scrutinised by the state. Normally we don't find it necessary to interfere with city business. We just rubber-stamp the city's approval ninety-nine times out of a hundred. But the authority to revoke a licence is still within the state's jurisdiction. As I say, we scarcely ever interfere. Am I making my point?'

'You are,' I said wearily.

Without a licence I would be a gone goose. These jokers had me over a barrel. I started talking about Lakecrest. They asked questions, shrewd, to-the-point questions. It lasted about thirty minutes. At the end of that time, either one of my two inquisitors could easily have been on that plane-ride with me in the morning. They knew as much about the Lakecrest episode as I did.

'Conspiracy,' Randall said finally. 'You, Steiner, Lorrimer and this witness, this Mrs. Monahan. I think we can swing a conspiracy indictment against the whole bunch of you.'

'You're forgetting the mayor,' I pointed out.

'I'm forgetting nothing. That special deputy joke was just a newspaper gag to get co-operation from the chief in Lakecrest.'

He stopped as he saw a blond crew-cut head wagging from side to side.

'No, sergeant, it won't do. I agree with your point of view,' conceded Brand, 'But we couldn't make such a charge good. The mayor may or may not have had some trivial excuse for appointing Preston a special deputy, but the fact remains that he did do it. He's not going to stand up in a courtroom and say as much. I'll go further. I'll venture an opinion that if you applied for a warrant you wouldn't get the district attorney's backing. All that will result will be some bad feeling between this department and the administration.'

He was right too. I was sure of it as he spoke, surer as I watched an expression of resignation spread over Randall's angry face. After a pause he said:

'Yup. I guess you're right, Mr. Brand. This is the kind of thing that's always liable to happen when you let the politician have power to interfere with police business. I don't like it, but I think you're right.'

Brand nodded.

'Mr. Preston, there are still a few questions I'd like to ask you. Mind, I'm only asking for opinions now. You can refuse to answer if you wish.'

After thirty minutes of the kind of questions this man could ask, plus the threat of losing my buzzer, I didn't think I would be refusing to answer.

'Go ahead,' I invited. 'Naturally, if I can help at all—'

Randall snorted. Even Brand managed a thin smile.

'You're already aware the police are looking for this man, Mo Shoeman? Do you think he's the right man?'

I chose my words carefully.

'I think the police are doing the right thing, yes. Shoeman is certainly out to kill Jingle, that much I know.'

'You know?' Brand elevated an eyebrow. 'This is interesting. The police are working only on reasoned assumption. Nobody has seen Shoeman since last night, or is my information out of date? In other words, Mr. Preston, how do you know?'

'Because I missed him by about half a minute not long ago.'

I told them what had happened at Whitney Blane's apartment.

'His sister?' Brand looked at Randall unlovingly. 'Were you aware of this relationship, Sergeant?'

Randall looked uncomfortable.

'No, sir, I was not. Remember, the only information I have about the guy is what the people at his office told me. He lives in a hotel, the staff there knew nothing about his private life. If the television crowd kept anything back about Shoeman, then I'm lost. They were my only source.'

'They don't seem to have been very helpful, do they?' observed the man from the state department. 'And you, Mr. Preston, you don't seem to have been very efficient.'

I was going to say, get out there and try, it, Brand. Let's see you out on that diamond, swinging the stick. Especially let's see you when Whitney Blane is pitching, so you keep forgetting about the ball. That's what I was going to say. What I did say was:

'I was just unlucky. At least I knew where to look.'

Randall tossed me a dirty look. Brand said hastily,

'Well, there's no use us falling out over what's done. We certainly have to pick up this Shoeman before he gets to Jingle. Tell me, Mr. Preston, what are your ideas about the missing woman, Alice Colfax?'

'I don't think she means anything at all,' I replied evenly. 'She's just a woman who had a rotten break, two in fact. If she's gone a little off her head and wandered away from home, I don't think it signifies. Give her a few days, she'll turn up again.'

'H'm,' he mused. 'You don't think it's an odd coincidence, that her husband should hold

197

the patent of a detonator which is widely used by our armed services. And that an explosive device was employed in Jingle's car?'

'Sure,' I admitted. 'It's an odd coincidence. That's exactly what it is, that and nothing else.'

'Preston is right,' Randall surprised me by saying. 'The guy we're after is Shoeman. This woman doesn't figure in the picture.'

Brand seemed to be satisfied. As near as anybody could judge from that impassive face.

'Very well. I appreciate your coming in here voluntarily, Mr. Preston, and I think you've been very frank with us. Needless to say, you will keep us closely informed of any developments.'

'Needless to say, you won't change your mind and tell me why you've come all the way down here to take a hand in this game?' I asked.

He smiled broadly.

'Needless to say,' he confirmed.

I thought it was time to pay a call on my employers.

CHAPTER FOURTEEN

The slanting rays of the early evening sun bounced richly off the silver buttons on the door-jockey's coat. He knew me this time, and I wondered whether he'd open the door. Last time all I got was good-morning. He smiled, a wide greeting.

'Evening, Mr. Preston.'

'Hi,' I told him as I approached.

He raised one white-gloved hand in a movement which may have had its origins in some rudimentary salute. But he still didn't open the door.

Inside the building I tried to feel for an atmosphere of tension, some additional hint of expectancy in the air. Nothing. Behind the white counter sat four girls. They all had coal-black hair, white silk blouses and red skirts. The telephones were still pink. I felt a momentary triumph over the artist who arranged the colour scheme for the benefit of visitors. Red skirts and pink telephones yet.

I leaned on the cold marble and the nearest one came over. She smiled at me in a warm and friendly way. It would have had more impact if she hadn't been looking over my shoulder most of the time.

'I work here,' I told her. 'Preston, special investigator with the Double Dee Jay show. Call Nicola Hardin and say I'm on my way up. And listen—'

I leaned further over the counter and spoke in a low tone. She had to bend down to catch what I said.

'Call me at once in Kingworth's private office if a man with a green beard tries to force his way upstairs.'

'I'll call Miss Hardin right away, Mr. Preston,' she assured me pleasantly. 'And I'll certainly warn you—hey—did you say a green beard—'

But I was already halfway to the elevators. I put a finger to my lips for silence. At least she was no longer looking over my shoulder. Upstairs the suspicious strong-arm character named Charlie let me in to the offices of the Double Dee Jay. He didn't offer to accompany me; so I headed straight for Nicola's room. On the way I passed a hard-eyed man who sat bolt upright in an armchair in the corridor. I'd seen him around at headquarters once or twice, and we nodded as I passed.

Nicola was sitting behind that empty desk again when I walked in.

'Miss Hardin,' I greeted. 'You are just as delicious as ever, and don't think I'm not noticing, but I'll check with you later. Right now I want to see Jingle.'

I nodded towards his door. She didn't smile.

'He's not here, Mark. You'd better see Mr. Kingworth.'

'I don't want Kingworth, honey. I want jingle. He has a broadcast in less than two hours so he can't be far away. How far?'

She picked up a telephone and deflected a key on the little plastic box in front of her.

'Mr. Preston has arrived, Mr. Kingworth. Shall I—yes, sir. At once.'

She put down the phone and stood up.

Although I was in a hurry I spared the two seconds it took to drink in the smooth flow of her restless body inside the yellow linen sheath.

'You're honoured, Mark. Mr. Kingworth will see you in the private suite. Not very many people get up that high.'

'It's already as much as I can manage to control my breathing,' I told her. 'How do I get to him?'

'I'll take you. Come on.'

She passed very close to me, too close. She knew I couldn't do anything about it at that moment because I had another appointment. It occurred to me briefly that maybe that was how Nicola Hardin progressed through the world. Always just that little bit out of reach.

She led me to what I thought was just another office door. It turned out to be a small elevator.

'Nice gag,' I observed.

'Mr. Kingworth uses this private elevator, so nobody on the public ones can find their way up to him by accident. Or, for that matter, by design.'

I didn't say anything. The elevator could hold two people comfortably enough. But when one of them was Nicola Hardin the other one had better keep his hands jammed in his pockets. Particularly if he was a slightly loose-living p.i. who had other fish to fry. We stepped out into a large room, sinking deep in the rich carpeting. Kingworth stood by a window staring out at what I knew had to be a wonderful view of the city. Standing up, he wasn't nearly so impressive, the legs looking thin and inadequate for the heavy work of supporting his bloated frame. He turned, nodded, and sat on a heavy wooden armchair that looked as if it might have seen service as a throne in some old Viking picture.

'Sit down, sit down,' he barked.

There were no more thrones. I parked in an easy chair, so did Nicola. I recorded this with mild surprise. I thought her part would have finished after she delivered me.

'You have unorthodox notions about working hours, Preston,' he rapped.

'I was doing some civic work,' I told him. 'The editor of the *Globe* promised to let you know what was going on.'

'Yes, yes, he phoned. When one of my employees stays off work, I expect him to have the courtesy to telephone in person.'

'I was on an airplane, Mr. Kingworth. Probably before you got out of bed this morning. I'm sorry if you're upset. There's nothing else I can say about it.'

'Well, there's something I can say about it,' he roared. 'Plenty in fact. But I haven't time now. Something you have to do, to earn your fantastic salary. Donny Jingle is missing. You'd better go and find him.'

'Missing? How missing?'

'He went out of this building at about-oh-what time was it, Miss Hardin?'

'Eleven thirty,' she contributed.

'Yes, at eleven thirty this morning. A few minutes later he telephoned to say he was going to hide himself away until the murderer had been caught. He's scared half to death.'

'I see.'

They watched me, the vice-president with impatience, Nicola with a kind of detached interest.

'Doesn't he have a broadcast tonight?' I queried.

'A sound broadcast, yes. Jingle's Jingles. Takes the air at eight p.m. Why?'

'Has he ever missed a programme before?'

'No, he hasn't, but what's that got to do with it?'

'He'll take a beating from the papers if they find out,' I mused. 'Public doesn't go for cowards.'

'Cowards?' he snorted. 'What nonsense is this? The man's life is in danger. There's a world of difference between a coward and a fool. Donny would be a fool if he made a public appearance the way things are.'

'What'll you do about the broadcast?' I asked.

'We always have a couple of taped programmes in hand, in case of sickness or anything like that. We'll use one of those.'

'I see. And what about the Double Dee Jay

tomorrow night? You got one of those on tape, too?'

'Tomorrow?' he faltered. 'Well I'm not even starting to think about tomorrow's show. This whole thing has to be cleared up before then. Shoeman can't hide from the entire police department for ever.'

'Glad you mentioned Shoeman, Mr. Kingworth. What makes everybody so sure he's the one?'

'Why, the police say so and that's good enough for me. He's vanished, too. Hardly what you'd expect from an innocent man.'

'Jingle's vanished too, according to what you tell me.'

'That's not the same thing at all,' he snapped. 'What are you trying to do, play with words, Preston?'

I shook my head.

'No. I'm just trying to fill in some of the gaps. There isn't very much I don't know about this business, Mr. Kingworth. But one thing that puzzles me is why everybody is so anxious to get Mr. Shoeman gassed for it.'

'Anxious?' he queried. 'I don't think I understand that word. And I don't like your tone.'

'He doesn't like my tone, Nicola,' I turned to her. 'Do you like my tone?'

'I don't know what you're talking about,' she replied, 'But I do know you're forgetting you're talking to Mr. Kingworth.'

I grinned, and turned back to the big boss.

'Nicola's very loyal to the network. She likes a big salary, and lots of expensive things. Told me so herself.'

'I think you've got something to say, Preston,' breathed the vice-president. 'I'll give you exactly one minute to say it, and then it will give me great pleasure to have you tossed out of this building.'

I laughed. I didn't feel particularly amused, but it seemed to me a laugh would probably irritate him more than any other reaction. And I wanted him irritated.

'Running a big operation like this, thinking in millions, that kind of thing distorts a man's viewpoint, wouldn't you say, Kingworth?'

He didn't reply, but the colour was gone from his flabby face. It now looked like unworked putty.

'Gives a man big ideas,' I went on. 'You know what somebody told me? Told me you had religion, and that religion was the network. Told me you were kind of a high priest. Well, he was wrong. You may have been a high priest, but you promoted yourself. Now you're God.'

Nicola got up.

'If you'd like me to leave, Mr. Kingworth—' she began.

'Sit down,' I snapped. 'I want you here.'

She sat down quickly.

'Don't look so worried, Kingworth,' I

consoled. 'If you're waiting for me to repeat the whole story; you're flattering me. The fact is, I don't know all the truth about this mess. Way it's shaping up, we may never know it all. The only man who could tell us is probably Mo Shoeman, and you've fixed him haven't you? He's the fall guy, the one who's going to take all the blame, while you're all as white and pure as the driven detergent ad. Only it isn't gonna work out quite so nice and clean. I know there's a bad smell here, and I give you my word, I'll turn it up.'

'I don't understand any of this,' said Kingworth, without conviction. 'Shoeman is the man who killed Chisum. The police think that, everybody here thinks it—'

'Don't be too sure about the police,' I interrupted. 'Sure, if you give them a lead, they'll follow it like a donkey follows a carrot. But they're not donkeys, they don't wear side-blinkers. They're kind of interested in everything else that goes on, without losing sight of the carrot. I may be a yard ahead of them at this minute, but that's only because I know one or two things they don't. Yet. They'll find out all right, and then they'll be up in this fine expensive office, asking questions. You won't be able to have them tossed out, Kingworth. They practise a rival religion, called the law, and they're fanatical about it. The first thing they'll ask you is how it came about everybody in this outfit forgot to mention Mo Shoeman was Whitney Blane's brother. Everyone was asked what they knew about the guy, but they all forgot to mention this one thing. Why?'

He licked his lips.

'It seemed a—a kindness. Poor Miss Blane did not have happy memories of the programme. There was no need for her to be involved in this unpleasantness. After all, nobody imagines she knows anything about it.'

I shook my head in sorrow.

'You're just not living in the same world as the rest of us, are you? Even if what you said were true, and it isn't, you still gave instructions to a number of people to withhold vital information from the police. Do you want another death on your hands?'

I shot the last question in almost as an afterthought. He started.

'I don't follow you.'

'Yes, you do. You mean you're trying not to think about it. Somewhere out there—' I waved towards the windows '—is Mo Shoeman. He has a gun and he's sworn to kill Donny Jingle. I heard him.'

The last part wasn't strictly true, but it had an effect.

'You heard him? When?'

'This afternoon. I almost grabbed him, when he was at a girl's apartment, but he got away. He's still roaming around.'

Vance Kingworth removed a dazzling

207

handkerchief from his breast pocket, and dabbed at the putty. His forehead gleamed with sudden wet.

'But this is terrible, terrible,' he muttered.

'Terrible,' I echoed. 'Also out in that same city, is your prize performer, Jingle. Just what is he doing, aside from asking to get himself killed?'

Kingworth cleared his throat and spoke in a dry whisper.

'He's gone to meet Shoeman. Has an appointment with him at seven forty-five.'

I checked my wrist quickly. It was five minutes after seven. Before I could speak again, the door of the private elevator opened suddenly. The tame gorilla, Charlie, came out pushing a woman in front of him. He had a blue revolver in his hand.

'Mr. Kingworth, sir. You said to come straight to you if anything happened. I caught this dame prowling around the Double Dee Jay suite. This was in her pocket!'

He waved the revolver. We all looked at the new arrival. She was of medium height, with soft honey-blonde hair that hadn't been attended to for days. Her face had a hang dog look, but through it you could see the now dissolved outlines of a once striking face. Her clothes were a shapeless bundle. She didn't speak or move, just stood there waiting for whatever was going to be done to her.

'Hallo, Alice,' I greeted softly.

She looked up quickly, the wide-set eyes searching for my face. Then she looked puzzled.

'You don't know me,' I reassured her, 'But in a way I was a friend of Ellie's.'

'Ellie's,' she repeated slowly, in a flat dispirited voice.

'Mr. Kingworth,' it seemed the right moment to restore the 'Mr.'

'—this woman needs attention and medical care. If you take my advice you'll see she gets it at the expense of A.I.C.T. Have Miss Hardin look after her, and call one of your own doctors. Charlie here can stick around, in case she tries anything. But you'll have to hurry. It's almost ten past seven.'

He nodded quickly. Years of making the right decisions in a hurry came to his aid.

'Do as he says, Nicola. Take her down to the special visitors lounge. Get a doctor, you know which one. Charlie, go with her and do whatever needs doing. And don't let anyone talk to her.'

Somehow they all squeezed into the small elevator. Alice Colfax held out a hand towards me, as if begging to be helped into a lifeboat, but Nicola coaxed her away.

Kingworth had gathered a little of his normal self-confidence from the incident.

'Well you had your own way. Would you mind telling me what this is all about. Who was that woman?'

209

'Name of Colfax,' I replied. 'Alice Colfax. She had a daughter, Ellie. The daughter left home, in a little town called Lakecrest, Nevada, and came to Monkton last week. So far as the police have been able to find out she only made contact with one person in this city. Dave Chisum. A few hours after she saw him she killed herself.'

'Killed herself?' he sounded querulous.

'Yes. Then her mother disappeared. Tonight she turned up here with a gun. She was going to kill Donny Jingle with it. That much I know.'

'Jingle? But I'm not with you at all. Why would she want to kill Donny?'

'I have a good idea, but that's all it is, an idea. Don't look so surprised, anyway. Seems to me the town is full of people who want to bump off this lovable guy. And—' I checked the watch again '—one of them is going to get his chance in just thirty minutes. Where?'

He nodded miserably.

'At the girl's apartment. Whitney Blane. You see—'

'Don't tell me now,' I cut in. 'There's no time. Later we can talk. Unless they put us in different cells, that is.'

He was still thinking about that when I left. Downstairs, I walked out to the visitors car space, climbed in the Chev and snapped open the glove compartment. A .38 police special has a certain beauty of its own under the right conditions. Mine looked beautiful to me, as I checked the clip and shoved it in the waistband of my pants.

Then I pressed the starter, and for a tenth of a second I went icy cold. For no reason at all I thought of Dave Chisum pressing another starter the night before, just a few yards from where I was sitting.

All that happened was the motor purred happily to life. Just the same I sat there a full half-minute, before easing off the brake and moving out into traffic.

Maybe it was some kind of presentiment. Maybe I wasn't going to die tonight.

But I had a feeling somebody was.

CHAPTER FIFTEEN

Once again I was standing outside Whitney Blane's door. Once again I was pressing the buzzer. Only this time I didn't get any results. I stared at the white panelling wondering what was waiting on the other side. The white panelling stared back without interest. I leaned my fore-finger against the door and it opened slightly. Somebody had fastened the catch in the open position. Cold fingers played kitten on the keys on my spine. The hair at the nape of my neck bristled, indication that I was afraid. I already knew it, without the indications.

Gently I pulled the .38 from my waist and my fear dissipated. Most of it. Kneeling down by the wall I pushed sharply with my foot. It swung easily open and—nothing. I sat there and strained my ears. Still nothing. Just soft music from the radio. One centimetre at a time I edged an eye round the side of the door. I saw the shoes first. They were brown and scuffed, and attached to a pair of legs which stuck out from behind a chair, I looked further, made out the crumpled figure of a man lying face down in the carpet. From the general build I thought the face would belong to Mo Shoeman. I inched into the room checking nervously into every space that might be big enough to conceal whoever put Mo on the floor. Finally I was satisfied we were alone. I went over and looked down at him. Then I stuck the .38 back in my pants and knelt beside him. Taking him gently by the shoulder I turned him over.

'Peek-a-boo,' he said.

In the hand which had been hidden under his body was a .45 Colt revolver. The direction it was pointing would have been an encouragement to anybody who happened to need a hole through his middle from front to back. Personally, I didn't care for it.

'We can't stay here like this all night,' he pointed out. 'Back up.'

I hesitated. He waggled the artillery.

'You're thinking I don't want to kill you. You're right. You're thinking I won't shoot. You're wrong. I'll put a bullet in your shoulder or your leg if you try to stop me. This is a point four five. The bullets are very heavy. They make big holes.'

I backed up. Shoeman scrambled to his feet.

'I see you have a gun, too. I thought of it first. Just drop yours on that chair.'

If he'd been nervous or excited I might have taken a chance. But he wasn't. Mo Shoeman was icy calm. He had something to do and it would be an unlucky day for anyone who got in his way. I watched sadly as the .38 slid down between the cushions.

'Good. Makes me feel easier,' he announced.

He walked over and pushed the door shut.

'Siddown, Preston. In a way, I'm glad to see you. You're the one man in this mess I care to talk to, right now.'

I sat down and helped myself to a smoke from an open box.

'Really? Why?' I asked.

'Everybody else is either A.I.C.T. or the law. You're somewhere in between.'

'I'm also a little bit of both,' I reminded him.

'Sure, yes, but you're not a real A.I.C.T. man, and you're not an authorised cop. Anyway,' he resolved the argument, 'You're the best I got. What's the time?'

'Seven forty. Why?'

'Got an appointment for seven forty-five.'

He came and sat where he could watch both me and the door without shifting.

'You're waiting for Jingle, that right?'

He nodded.

'When he gets here, you're going to kill him. You made a mess of it last night, and Dave Chisum died instead. So now you're going to make it good.'

He shook his head.

'That's what everybody thinks, I know. But I didn't kill Dave. It was an accident.'

'Sure, he died accidentally. But you were trying to kill Jingle, so it's still murder.'

He put the Colt in his lap.

'Preston, you are looking at the All-American sucker in the king-size pack. I'm going to tell you what really happened. That way you might get somebody to believe it one day. What was that?'

He grabbed up the gun and trained it on the door. I didn't hear anything, and after a minute of tense silence he slowly lowered the heavy weapon.

'What do you know about Donny?' he demanded.

'Not much that's to his credit. He doesn't seem to have a lot of friends.'

'You can whistle that in C major,' he retorted. 'Everybody in this business hates that guy all the way down to his shoestrings.'

'But nobody else is going to kill him,' I pointed out. 'Only you hate him that much.'

'No,' he shook his head. 'You're wrong there. Plenty of people hate him that much. But I'm elected because I'm already dead. Best I can expect is the gas chamber, because of Dave. So I haven't a single thing to lose. Jingle has got A.I.C.T., Kingworth and a million dollars worth of advertising behind him. I can't fight him with the truth. Only with this.'

He tapped at the cold black barrel.

'What is the truth, Mo?'

I wanted to keep him talking. Keep inching my fingers towards the gap in the cushions where the .38 nestled.

'The truth? The truth is ridiculous. Nobody tried to kill anybody last night. At least I didn't think so. Now I'm beginning to wonder. The whole thing was a stunt. Donny is crazy for stunts, always getting up to some new gimmick to keep the Double Dee Jay show right in the public eye. And, let's face it, the guy has a talent for it.'

'All right, I'm facing it. Tell me about the stunt.'

He didn't answer for a moment, listening intently for some imaginary sound on the other side of the door.

'Eh? Oh, yes. The publicity gag. Donny got this idea about having his life threatened. Wrote a couple of crazy notes to himself, planted that slug in the wall of his house. One

215

or two things like that.'

'Who was in on this? Everybody?'

He chuckled grimly.

'Oh, no. Not everybody. Donny explained to me we could never make the gag stick if everybody knew. So nobody did. Except me. Me and Donny.'

'How about Kingworth? He doesn't strike me as a man who'd appreciate people keeping little secrets from him.'

'You're right. I was scared about V.K. but Donny told me not to worry. After all, he was the star. Without him, the network might not exactly collapse, but it would feel the money pains. He wouldn't have anybody in on the gag but me. And if it all went off O.K. he guaranteed me a fifty a week raise. It seemed an easy way to get a big raise, so I played along.'

I was starting to hear things outside myself, the way people always do if they're expecting sounds.

'Didn't you wonder why he needed you at all?' I queried. 'After all, just the little things he wanted doing could be done by one man.'

'Now you tell me,' he agreed sadly. 'All except the bomb. Donny needed an expert for that. That was the pay-off. Donny was going to have a narrow escape from death. Then, when the questions started coming, it would all come out. The way he'd been bravely carrying on despite all these threats and like that.

216

Everybody else on the show would have to tell how they'd been sworn not to spill about the threats. Donny would be quite a little hero. Joe Public drinks up that show-must-go-on bit like it was old brandy.'

'I see,' I breathed. 'So Dave Chisum went out to the car; didn't know about the gag, and the gag blew up in his face.'

'Be your age, Preston. Donny sent Dave out there. He'd been doing it several nights straight. I didn't know about that. Donny's a great one for having little secrets. So he has a little secret with me about a phoney attempted murder. Then he has a little secret with Dave about Dave wearing his clothes, and driving home in his car every night. He doesn't tell me about Dave and he doesn't tell Dave about the bomb, and suddenly Dave is dead. That's murder, Preston. Donny killed Dave. Only he had it done by what-do-you-call it? Proxy. Yeah, proxy. That's me.'

He grinned again mirthlessly.

'What's the time?'

'Seven fifty,' I told him.

'Guy's late. He said seven forty five.'

'I'm not too bright sometimes,' I told him. 'But would you mind letting me know why Jingle should come here to meet you? He might guess you'll bring that with you.'

I pointed to the Colt. Mo shook his head.

'No reason he should. If I hadn't got lucky last night I'd have been waiting here without this. The prize pigeon.'

'Lucky?'

'Sure. After Dave—after it happened, I nearly went out of my head. I wasn't normal for a few minutes. Donny pulled me together. He got me alone, told me to get a grip on. myself. It was an accident. He'd get Kingworth and the whole network behind me, and it would come out all right. But he'd need time. It wouldn't be possible to set up a thing like that in five minutes, which was about all the time we'd have before the police arrived. He'd need most of a day. I'd have to get through any questions the police asked me, which wouldn't be too hard. I'd only be one of a dozen people, and it would only mean routine questions. Then I'd drop out of sight, so the police wouldn't be able to get at me for any real tough grilling before he'd had a chance to set up the network law-boys. After all, he reminded me, we were in this thing together. He'd be fighting for himself as well as me. I'm better than half-smart as a rule, but I'd been the cause of a man's death a few minutes earlier. I wasn't thinking my best, so I agreed.'

He sighed and pulled at his nose.

'What happened to make you think it wasn't such a good idea?' I prompted.

'It was later. Before the cops came. There was just Kingworth, the script boys and Nicola around, outside of Donny and me. He went into Dave's office with Kingworth. I guessed

218

he was going to tell V.K. what had happened. I went into Nicola's room. The partition in there is thin, you can hear conversation if there isn't too much studio noise—I mean background noise.'

My fingers were now directly over the crack in the cushions and not more than four inches from the .38.

'And you heard Donny, your protector, feed you to the lions.'

'Damn right. I couldn't believe it. Know what he said?

'He said "V.K. I've got something terrible to tell you. I know who murdered Dave. It was Shoeman." Kingworth asked him how he knew and he told him some yarn about Whit—my sister—told him she telephoned about an hour before it happened and warned him. According to Donny, I stormed out of her place on my way to kill him. She doesn't love him too well herself, but she didn't want me a murderer just the same. So Donny said he took it seriously enough to get a gun from Charlie and put it in the drawer of his desk. He didn't tell Charlie what it was for, in case it turned out I was talking a lot of hot air, but he wanted to be ready for me if I meant it.'

'Just a minute,' I chipped in. 'That bit about borrowing Charlie's gun, that can be checked.'

He nodded morosely.

'It has been. I asked Charlie about it, and he told me Donny asked for it about ten o'clock.

219

Said he seemed a bit upset about something,'

'I see. You were telling me about Donny's yarn to Kingworth. How did he explain about Dave?'

'Oh, that wasn't hard. Dave was just going through the usual routine they'd been using since the threats started. Dave wouldn't have anything to fear from me, because naturally that gag with the overcoat and hat wouldn't make me think he was Jingle, the way a stranger might. I'd know either of them anywhere. So he didn't think Dave was running any more than the usual risk. It never occurred to him that the car itself could be a danger. You shoulda heard him. Donny's always saying he wants to make a movie, play a straight part. I'm able to testify, on the show he did for Kingworth last night, the man would be in line for an award.'

It was a neat frame. I asked:

'What was Kingworth's reaction?'

'Typical. Not a word about Dave. Only questions about what was best for the network. There were three people besides me who knew about it, Donny told him. Donny himself, Kingworth and my sister, Whitney. The first thing to do was keep the police from catching up with her too fast. The crew ought to be told to leave her out of any statement they made to the police. Then he'd go and see her, explain what the network was doing for me, tell her to keep out of it.'

'Going too fast, Mo,' I said. 'What was the network supposed to be doing for you?'

'Ah, yes. This is where Donny played it very smart indeed. If you knew the guy, you'd realise just how like him the next bit was. Nobody could feel more than he did about Dave, but the man was dead, and nothing could bring him back. What they had to consider, Donny and Kingworth, was the living. All the people in the show, the sponsors, the shareholders. Do right by Dave's family of course, even better than right. But we couldn't stand the kind of public reaction we'd get to a killer right on the team. The legal department would have to think something up, even provide me with an alibi if they had to. He bore me no animosity, he said. He wouldn't get any personal satisfaction out of seeing me found guilty, not if it meant so many other people losing their jobs. In fact, he had a kind of crazy idea which might be the way out, but it was so off beat he hardly liked to suggest it.'

'So Kingworth insisted he should.'

'Sure. Anybody ever tell you what a real gone creep Donny can be?'

'I've heard one or two suggestions in that direction,' I admitted.

'Well, hold on to your hat,' advised Shoeman. 'This crazy suggestion he hardly liked to mention was the truth. He told the vice-president he was prepared to get up and swear he'd arranged the whole thing with me as a publicity gag. It went wrong, and Dave died. Of course he couldn't say exactly how that would leave us legally, but with all the money the network spent on legal talent, we ought to be able to get away with it.'

I found myself nodding in something like admiration. Horrified admiration.

'I begin to see what everybody means about this guy,' I told Shoeman. 'He really is on the slippery side, isn't he?'

'In spades,' he returned. 'Anyway Kingworth swallowed all this boloney. He said it wasn't possible to make a firm decision right then about what was to be done. Two things were certain. I'd have to get out of sight, and Whit would have to be told what was going on. Jingle said he'd see to all that. Kingworth started to say what arrangements there'd be for today, then Nicola walked in and I had to clear out.'

'You think she could tell you were listening to their conversation?' I queried.

'I don't know. I got out of there pretty fast, I was in a blue sweat, Preston. Maybe she noticed. At that moment I couldn't have cared if she'd seen me wiring up Donny's car.'

'So what happened after that?

'Well, I hung around a while then Donny came and found me, and gave me this pitch about getting out of sight. He gave me two hundred and told me to find some place where

I could stay the night and most of today. Suggested I use a different name. Kingworth was holding a meeting this morning to decide what our legal position was, and until that was all sewed up tight, he didn't want me getting any rough handling by the police. I was naturally in a state of something like shock. I might go and say a lot of things I couldn't retract later. The network was going to see me through, but I'd have to co-operate and do whatever Kingworth wanted, else I might foul it up. Nobody was to know where I was, not even Donny. But he would meet me here tonight. At seven forty five. What's the time?'

'Seven fifty-nine. Look, I can see you're in trouble, plenty of trouble, but you think you're going to solve anything by killing Jingle? Certainly, he's framed you for Chisum's death, but he's also giving you an out. If Kingworth is lining up all those lawyers over there, I'd say you have a very good chance of a light sentence. Maybe even acquittal. Sure you hate Jingle's guts, and you've a right to. But is it worth dying for? Because if you kill him now, you're going to the gas-chamber, Mo.'

The dry tongue darted nervously over his lips again.

'You still don't quite get it, do you, Preston? I have to kill him. If I don't he's going to kill me. That's what he's coming here for. I'm the only one alive who can possibly know he meant Dave Chisum to die in that car last night. Donny murdered Dave. I was just the sucker who provided the materials. The amount of nitro I put under that hood was only enough to make a loud noise and blow up the engine. Donny must have put a few more sticks in there himself. You can steal it from any construction site. I've had nearly twenty-four hours to work this all out. Donny has to kill me. Kingworth won't like it, but Donny'll play for hero. He came here to ask Whit if she knew where I was, and I started shooting at him. Even A.I.C.T. couldn't expect Jingle to stand there while I killed him in cold blood. So I get dead, and he's in the clear.'

The radio music suddenly stopped. A man's voice said:

'Eight o'clock on Friday night and time for Jingle's Jingles. And here in person is your favourite man-about-music, top of the turntable, the fabulous D-J of A.I.C.T.'s Double Dee Jay Show, Donny Jingle.'

Crescendo studio applause, then Jingle's voice,

'Hallo and how-do. We won't delay, let's start the day with—'

Mo swung round towards the radio in disbelief.

'It can't be,' he protested, 'He has to come here and kill me.'

'Right,' said a new voice. Jingle's.

Everything happened fast.

Jingle was framed in the doorway, a wicked-

224

looking automatic in his hand. Shoeman was still turned towards the radio. Jingle fired before Shoeman could bring his arm round. I clutched desperately for the .38, falling to the ground at the same time. The first slug missed Shoeman completely and winged its vicious way into the wall behind. The second was better, hitting him in the shoulder as he started to rise. It spun him half-round and as he fell to the floor, the automatic in Jingle's hand jumped again and Shoeman screamed as the slug went home. There was another shot as Shoeman's hand gripped convulsively at the trigger of the Colt, and an ounce of lead smashed harmlessly into the carpet. So far these two were not concerned with me. Now I brought up the .38, lining it at jingle's chest. A shot, but not from me. Jingle swayed, leaned against the door, the automatic slipping from his grasp. I didn't know who the new gun-artist was, so I stayed on the floor.

'Police,' said a man's voice behind the disc-jockey. 'Everybody in there drop your guns and walk out with your hands way up.'

It was Randall. I'd never much cared for Randall's voice before. Now I found it filled me with a warm friendliness. I put the .38 away and walked to the door. Jingle was holding one hand to his side. Carefully I kicked the automatic past him and out into the hall. I wanted to kick him too, but I didn't. I put my hands on my head and walked out. Randall,

Brand and a uniformed sergeant looked at me with quick suspicion, guns ready.

'Oh, no,' groaned Randall.

'Anybody else inside?' asked Brand.

'Mo Shoeman, but he's no danger. Jingle shot him twice.'

Randall and the sergeant went in cautiously. Brand slipped his gun into a shoulder-holster. There was an acrid smell of cordite in the hall.

'You shoot Jingle?' I asked.

He nodded.

'I'm not so mixed up in local politics, as your own department. Shooting somebody like Donny Jingle is not likely to win a man any big friends in this city. It was better coming from me.'

'It was great coming from anybody,' I assured him. 'That guy came here to kill.'

'Yes,' he agreed. 'I'm ashamed to say he took us by surprise, there. We thought he was just coming to meet somebody, probably Shoeman. We were right behind, but he just kicked open the door and started shooting. Is Shoeman dead?'

'No.' Randall answered the question as he came back to join us. 'Jingle may be a hell of a disc-jockey, but he's a rotten shot. Shoeman got one in the shoulder, one in the leg. In two weeks he'll be ready for the gas-chamber.'

'No,' I contradicted. 'It's a long story, but Shoeman isn't guilty of anything much except a little stupidity and a natural desire to save his skin. Jingle's your killer.'

Two more uniformed officers appeared in the hall. Randall motioned them into the apartment.

'We know about Jingle,' rejoined Brand. 'How is he, by the way, sergeant?'

'Got a nasty wound in his side. He'll survive it. There's an ambulance on its way. Preston, let's all go inside, and hear some of that long story you were talking about.'

'Could it wait till tomorrow?' I protested. 'I'm feeling weak, after all a man was going to kill me just now.'

Randall smiled, a wide unfriendly smile.

'You'll make me blubber all over this nice carpet,' he assured me. 'Now get in there and start talking.'

'It would be interesting, Mr. Preston,' Brand suggested.

I thought about my licence again and went back into Whitney's apartment. The sergeant had made Shoeman as comfortable as he could without moving him. The little man had lost quite a bit of blood and was out cold. Jingle lay back in a chair, drawing deep, shuddering breaths. His face was blotchy grey. Randall looked down at him with a professional's appraisal.

'If the ambulance gets here inside fifteen minutes, he'll make it,' pronounced the sergeant.

There seemed to be blood everywhere.

Blood and wounded men. The place was like a battlefield. Randall sat down and lit a cigarette. Brand and I exchanged glances, then we sat too. Nobody felt like talking It was an eerie five minutes before the ambulance came. With them came the police M.E., a bustling busy man in his late fifties. He took in the scene at a glance, tut-tutted and started with Jingle. We all watched as he made a quick examination of each man, then handed them over to the white-coated attendants. As they helped him on to the stretcher, Jingle passed out.

The doctor scuttled over to where we were sitting, writing quickly on a pad which was clipped to a piece of board.

'Not very pretty, not very pretty,' he chirped at Randall. 'These the men responsible?'

He waved a hand at Brand and a weary private investigator.

'No, doc.'

Randall explained who we were and the M.E. stopped bustling long enough to look a little red around the ears. Then he excused himself, promised to have a report to Homicide within an hour and went out. Bustling.

Randall then dismissed the uniformed men and the three of us were alone.

'Peace, it's wonderful,' said Randall. 'I guess we may have as much as half an hour of it before the newshounds get on to all this.

Preston, you have the floor. Tell us about Shoeman.'

I told them. All of it this time, no holdouts.

'One or two things in there you coulda mentioned earlier, Preston. Might have saved all this Jesse James act in there,' observed Randall.

I wasn't going to bite on that. Brand said,

'You think Shoeman was telling the truth?'

'I'm sure of it,' I replied. 'You going to charge him, sergeant?'

'Why ask me? I'm not the D.A. If the story checks, maybe not. But still maybe yes, don't forget that. I can't speak for the District Attorney.'

'If Shoeman's story is true,' continued Brand, 'It relies on Jingle wanting Chisum dead in the first place. Why would he want that d'you suppose?'

I brought out my pack and flicked out an Old Favourite.

'That's one thing we may never know for certain,' I told him. 'But I have a lot of ideas about it if you're interested.'

'I'd like to hear them,' he suggested.

'All right. Before he came to the big city and hit the main lode, Jingle was a small-time radio voice in Nevada. His name was Chuck Matthews those days. His buddy, even then, was the same Dave Chisum. Matthews was no contender for the Sweet American Boy title. By all accounts the man was a one hundred per cent S.O.B.'

Brand raised an eyebrow but did not interrupt.

'These two used to work at a lot of small stations. One of them was in a town called Lakecrest. The people there don't have beautiful memories of Matthews. About four years back, there was a nasty crime in Lakecrest. A fifteen year old girl was raped. Last week she came here to Monkton City to kill herself. Her name was Ellie Colfax. One of the last people to see her alive was Dave Chisum. So far I've been telling you facts. Now I'm only guessing. Ellie's mother, Alice, was a very good-looking woman married to a man years older. Her husband says he doesn't remember Matthews, but the way he said it, I don't believe him. I think Matthews is the one who raped Ellie. I think she kept quiet about him because he told her he was having an affair with her mother, and the shock of it all might be more than her father could stand. I also think the father had some idea about Matthews and Alice Colfax even if he couldn't prove anything. Certainly he didn't know it was Matthews who raped Ellie.'

'What makes it certain?' interposed Randall.

'Because Joe Colfax is like you or me or the next man,' I told him. 'If he knew it was Matthews he would have killed him.'

'Maybe,' Randall acknowledged grudgingly.

230

'What makes all of this any reason for Matthews to want Chisum dead?'

'Don't forget I'm only guessing,' I reminded him. 'My guess is that Dave Chisum knew nothing about it until Ellie contacted him last week. When he found out he couldn't take it. He'd stood for the blackmail, the kick-backs, the way Matthews, or jingle as he now is, the way he pushed everybody around. But this was different. I'm guessing he threatened jingle with the law and jingle felt he couldn't risk that threat being carried out.'

Brand shook his head.

'Not quite. Some very pretty guessing up to a point. But on motive you're wrong.'

'Oh? There seems to be something I don't know?' I made it a question. Randall snorted.

'Something you don't know? The nerve of you guys. You spend your whole lives in bars and dames apartments and think you're Sherlock Holmes, all you p.i.'s. You're right, there's something you don't know, and that something is practically everything. We have a police department in this town, mister, and it has a record at least as good as yours for solving crimes. You gonna tell the big brain here, about some of the things he don't know, Mr. Brand?'

Brand smiled equably.

'You're wrong about Chisum only threatening to go to the police, Mr. Preston. He did go. Before I go into that, let me tell you something about Ellie Colfax. She was a very sweet gentle girl, who'd been brought up to lead a rather sheltered life. After she was attacked, that all changed. She became broody, suffered from long bouts of melancholia. In these depressive periods; her own doctor says, and don't forget he'd known her all her life, that she had positive suicidal tendencies. Only one thing stood between Ellie and the taking of her own life. That was her mother's condition. The mother lived only for Ellie, and was herself seriously ill mentally for a long time, years in fact. Only Ellie could do anything with her. It was this need of her mother's that kept Ellie going. Then a couple of months ago, her mother began to pull out of it, actually began to improve. The doctor says it was a minor miracle, and only Ellie's strength and devotion had made it possible.' Brand coughed slightly, excused himself and went out in the kitchen to get a drink of water. Randall winked.

'This is a good opportunity for you, Preston. You can latch on to a free view of how real police officers work.'

'Thanks,' I said drily.

Brand came back, and sat down to get on with his story.

'Now where was I? Oh, yes. Mrs. Colfax began to get well. This had an inverted effect on Ellie. She started to go downhill again. The doctor was watching her as much as he could.

It seemed as if her mother's recovery removed the barrier that had stood between Ellie and suicide. He tried to get her to go away for treatment. Naturally the parents were all in favour, and Ellie finally agreed. Then, the day before she was due to leave for the hospital she left home. She came here, as we know, but nobody knew that at the time. After a number of attempts to contact Jingle she realised it was hopeless. The man had a whole army of people whose job it was to see he wasn't bothered. Then she had a brainwave. She telephoned and left a message to say that if he didn't call her back within one hour she'd go to the police.'

'Who took the message?' I asked.

'It was passed to Miss Hardin, as Jingle's private secretary. She gets a lot of screwy calls, but she thought this one might be worth mentioning to Chisum. Chisum wasn't too impressed either, but a phone call doesn't cost much. After he talked with her, he realised there might be some real trouble brewing. Jingle wasn't around, so Chisum went over to see the girl himself. Not that he believed what she'd said, but he wanted to know what she was up to. When he saw her, talked with her, he soon I realised her story was genuine. He remembered the rape case, because he and Matthews had been in Lakecrest at the time. What clinched it though, for Chisum, was Ellie's mother, Alice. Chisum had known about Matthews and Alice Colfax. To him that was just another hay-rolling, nothing to work up any excitement over. But now he was dealing with something different. This was something unspeakable, obscene. Chisum wasn't going to hush this one up. He never cared much for Jingle. When he covered up the fight and the dirty behaviour he did it for the money. You were right when you said Chisum stood for plenty. But this was the big one, and he wasn't going to keep quiet about it.'

'What did Ellie want exactly?' I asked.

Brand shrugged.

'You have to remember she was by this time a very disturbed girl. She said all she wanted was for Jingle to go and see her. She wanted the big famous television star to call at her place, Ellie Colfax's place. She wanted to look at him, listen to him, then order him out. Just that, nothing else. Chisum thought it was crazy. He wanted her to go to the police with him right then, but she wouldn't. Said she had to think about her family still. The only thing she wanted was to make Jingle crawl, then she'd be satisfied. Chisum said he'd try to fix it up, then left. He went to police headquarters and had an interview with a lieutenant there. The lieutenant took him to see the inspector. The inspector knew this was a very hot potato, and he brought in the assistant commissioner. Chisum got a bit angry. To him the whole thing was an open and shut criminal case. He didn't know how carefully the police have to proceed in a matter of this kind. There were big names tied up with Mr. Donny Jingle. Big names and big money. All that adds up to, big pull, as you may have heard.'

It's been mentioned,' I nodded.

'Up at the capitol, we have a small department of people who advise in matters of this kind. We don't interfere unless we're invited, but we do specialise in police matters where there is some possibility of political interference with the process of law. The assistant commissioner thought, and I agree with him, that this was something in our backyard. Chisum thought the police would send a car out for Jingle with the sirens screaming. The rest of us thought we'd have several days of careful background work to do before we could move with some measure of certainty. I arranged to come down the next morning to get the ball rolling. Only next morning it was too late. Ellie Colfax killed herself a few hours after she talked with Chisum. Why, we'll never know. She could have done it any time in the past four years. The police doctor studied her history, and he thinks it could have been the emotional upheaval of having talked with Chisum. Don't forget, the girl had kept all that locked up inside her for four years. Anyway, whatever the cause, Ellie was dead. We had no case.'

'You had Chisum's evidence—' I began.

'No evidence at all,' he countered. 'Just a hearsay report of a conversation with a girl who was known to be mentally ill. But there was something else. A certain senator, whose name you could no doubt bring to mind, has been agitating for months for a thorough investigation into what he likes to call the morass of the entertainment industry. Personally, I think he's one of these blowhards who likes to make a lot out of a little. You know, one dancer gets drunk, and the whole business is riddled with alcoholics.'

'I've met the type,' I agreed. 'And I think I know who you mean. But I don't quite see where he fits in with any of this.'

'If you'd stop interrupting Mr. Brand, Preston, maybe you'd be able to follow a little easier,' said Randall pointedly.

I shut up.

'Chisum took it very badly that we weren't able to proceed against Jingle. That girl really got to him, maybe because he had a little girl of his own. I offered him a kind of second prize. Asked if he'd feed me material for a state prosecution against Jingle on some of his other activities. None of us felt like letting Jingle get off scot-free. In fact, although I shouldn't say this in my job, some of us felt quite vindictive towards him.'

'And Jingle must have found out what Dave was doing.'

236

'Correct. We had no doubt the great d-j was responsible for Chisum's death, but it was going to take an awful lot of unpicking. Shoeman was our break.'

I sighed.

'Ah yes. Mo Shoeman. How about him?'

Brand looked across at Randall.

'It's really a matter for your city police department now,' he replied.

Randall stared at us unblinkingly.

'Sergeant,' I said, 'And you too, Mr. Brand. Let us now talk over a certain proposition.'

CHAPTER SIXTEEN

The ape-like Charlie admitted me to the Double Dee jay offices at the A.I.C.T. building.

'You must be somebody real special,' he greeted me. 'Every reporter in town and half the sponsors are trying to get up here. But you get in. And Mr. Kingworth in person is going to talk to you.'

'Wrong, Charlie,' I shook my head. 'Mr. Kingworth is going to listen. I am going to talk and he is going to listen. If he doesn't, tomorrow you and Mr. Kingworth will have something in common. You'll both be out of a job.'

He didn't get it. He walked me round to

Nicola Hardin's office and then went away. She looked very beautiful across the desk, her troubled face only adding to the attraction.

'Mr. Kingworth is waiting,' she said formally. 'I'll take you up to him.'

'Before we go, how is Alice Colfax?' I demanded.

She looked at me carefully.

'As well as can be expected. Mr. Kingworth is arranging for special rest treatment in a private sanatorium. The poor woman is not herself. She's been saying awful things.'

'Like true things, for instance?' I jibed.

'Naturally, nobody believes anything she's saying,' she faltered. 'But nevertheless, Mr. Kingworth doesn't want that sort of talk to be misreported.'

'Sure,' I agreed. 'Or even accurately reported. Especially accurately.'

Nicola flushed.

'I don't know why you choose to be rude to me, Mark. I only do what I'm told here, like everyone else.'

We were at the private elevator now. I made no reply as we ascended to Kingworth's office/apartment or what-have-you.

The vice-president was huddled behind the vast desk. He seemed to have lost a lot of size somewhere, looked shrunken somehow. Even the once-bushy eyebrows seemed bedraggled.

'I have your message, Preston. If half of what you told Miss Hardin over the telephone is true—'

'It's all true.' There's more besides. Oh, don't go, Nicola—' She'd been about to step back into the elevator. Now she looked to Kingworth as always for instructions.

'And don't look at him,' I snapped irritably. 'I'm calling the tune around here. It may be only for ten beautiful minutes but I'm going to squeeze all the gravy out of every one. Sit down over there.'

Kingworth did not interfere. That surprised Nicola. She sat down over there and I started talking. I talked about Lakecrest, Nevada, and Dave Chisum. About Jingle and Mo Shoeman and a lot of things. Finally I said:

'Well, that's almost the whole story.'

'Terrible,' Kingworth wobbled his flabby face from side to side. 'A terrible, terrible story. This is an awful blow to the network. We'll be a long time repairing all this damage. I suppose there is no possibility, in your professional opinion, of Donny getting off? Remember, we have a legal department here which—'

'Which will do nothing to help him,' I finished. 'They won't lift a finger.'

'You're wrong there, Preston. When one of my people is in trouble, I know how to fight—'

He made an attempt to regain his normal bristling authority, but it was a poor try. His voice died away as he looked at my shaking head.

'Up to a point, I'm with you,' I told him. 'One of your people is in trouble, and you are going to toss in everybody in the state of California who has a legal qualification to get him off the hook. But it isn't Jingle. It's Mo Shoeman. And don't interrupt, I'm not finished yet. You have been caught out in two criminal acts in the past twenty-four hours, Kingworth. Not the network, not the sponsors, just you personally. I don't know who you think you are. You get the running of a big outfit like this, control the lives of a lot of people and suddenly you get a God-complex. You even move up here on the roof of the world, but it doesn't make it true, you know. God is still on the next floor up. You've been a big man around here so long you forget sometimes there's a world outside. A world where most of the people never heard of you. A world where you can break the law if you want to. But you have to pay, just like any poor slob. Well, you're going to pay. But even now, you get a break. The slob would go to jail. You could go too, but it wouldn't prove anything. So you're going to do a few little things instead.'

'I don't know what you're driving at,' he mumbled. 'I didn't break any laws.'

'Then you're beginning to crack up, Kingworth. Your memory's fading. Let me remind you what you did. You conspired with the people here to withhold vital information

240

from the police in a case of homicide. Not just conspired, you ordered the others to do it. Told 'em not to mention that Whitney Blane was Mo Shoeman's sister. That delayed the police in getting at the truth. If jingle or Shoeman dies, that will be as much your fault as anybody elses. The other thing though, that's the hole card. You were told by jingle that Shoeman was the murderer, and you instructed him to keep quiet about it.'

'There was no harm in that,' he argued. 'Shoeman wasn't guilty, was he?'

'No,' I agreed. 'He wasn't. But you didn't know that. He could just as well have been guilty as anybody else. Yet you kept the police in the dark about that, too. They aren't very friendly towards you right now.'

'It was all done for the best. I have a lot of responsibility here. People's jobs, all the capital that's tied up. You don't realise.'

'Try convincing a jury,' I told him. 'They'll be twelve of the people you have such little regard for around here. Joe Public, the chumps. Try telling them why you thought it was O.K. to turn a man loose on the streets when you had every reason to believe he was a murderer. Joe Public has a wife, maybe kids loose in the city. He doesn't like to think they might come up against a killer who's been allowed to roam around because you don't want to embarrass the stockholders.'

I was not on very firm ground here, and I

241

was relying on the fact that Kingworth had had all he could take for one day. He raised an arm in despair, and it looked as if I had him.

'You're very good at telling me how much trouble I'm in. It would be more help if you suggested what I could do about it.'

It was only a remark. He wasn't expecting any suggestions. From where he sat there was only darkness. I had a surprise for him.

'The police are not anxious to go ahead on the rape case,' I began. 'It would only cause further unnecessary suffering for the Colfax family. Also, they have to prosecute Shoeman on the evidence they have. They don't like to do it but they haven't much choice. You're a different case. They don't have to do anything about you at all unless they choose. It would be a long and expensive trial for the taxpayers. At the end, you may even get off. Crime-wise, that is. I've no doubt the good old network would give you the fast goodbye. Have you?'

He didn't answer, but the look on his face was enough.

'I think I can represent to the police that you acted under strain,' I went on. 'If I can show them what an upstanding citizen really are, they'll probably decide they ought not to waste the taxpayer's money on a prosecution.'

His eyes took on a crafty look. He could smell a deal now, and a deal was something he understood.

'And just how do you propose to convince them of that?'

'Not me,' I contradicted. 'You. You're going to convince them. You're going to provide Shoeman's defence. Whether you pay or the network I don't give a damn, but that courtroom's going to be bulging at the seams with your lawboys. That's one thing.'

'Ah. There are others?'

'Two is Mrs. Colfax. Nicola tells me you're having her sent to a private sanatorium. You do that, and keep her there till she's well again. Three, there's Whitney Blane. Her voice is no worse than plenty of others who get on your screens regularly. All she ever did wrong was have Jingle go sour on her. Put her back on the payroll. She's had little enough out of all this so far except misery.'

I stopped talking. Kingworth waited a moment, then he said:

'You're forgetting four.'

'Four?'

'Certainly. Point number four. Shoeman, Mrs. Colfax, Whitney. That's only three. Nothing there is very much of a strain on the resources. Now we have to come to you, don't we? The big slice of the cake?'

As his confidence crept back he began to expand again. I swear he was already bigger than when we started talking.

'You forget, Kingworth, I'm an employee here. All my services come in with the daily ticket. One hundred bucks a day. I don't expect to be paid twice for the same job.'

He looked at me suspiciously, saw I meant it, then changed his expression to puzzlement.

'You mean it don't you?'

'I mean it.'

He nodded, picked up the cherrywood pipe from its place on the table and sniffed at the bowl.

'About the police, you're sure you can do what you say? I've always heard the police don't make deals.'

'The police sometimes have to decide what's best in the public interest,' I informed him. 'That isn't the same thing.'

'All right.'

He'd made up his mind. I felt a sense of triumph. Not the big victory I'd been savouring when I first arrived. Somehow there wasn't much kick to pushing around a frightened little fat man. I turned to Nicola Hardin, who hadn't spoken the whole time.

'Can I trust him?'

'You can trust him,' she affirmed. 'If Mr. Kingworth gives his word nothing else needs to be said.'

'O.K.'

I walked to the elevator. Behind me Kingworth spoke.

'Preston, I've been thinking over your employment here. We don't really have a need for anyone like you. Not any more. I'm giving you ten days' notice to terminate. And, as you've been so busy, take ten days' vacation from work.'

I turned and grinned. He managed something of a grin in reply.

Nicola came down in the elevator. We went back in her office. She was elated.

'Well that was quite a little show you put on, Mark. What happens now?'

'Now? Between us, you mean?'

She nodded, and her eyes were shining.

'Nothing, angel. Nothing happens for us at all. You were right when I first saw you. You're too rich for my blood. When you said you had a keen appreciation of a dollar, I didn't realise how deep it went.'

'I don't understand,' she said quietly. 'What are you trying to say?'

'We just don't go together, honey. A gal looking after herself is one thing but you take it too far. You were one of the people who forgot to tell the police or me about Mo and Whit Blane.'

'But that was on instructions from Mr. Kingworth himself,' she protested.

'Sure. And I was with Mo tonight when Jingle put two bullets in him. That wasn't on Kingworth's instructions, it was Jingle's own idea. But if you'd helped the police last night Mo would have been in a cell. It might not have been very comfortable but he wouldn't have needed any blood transfusions either.'

245

She coloured slightly.

'Naturally I could have no idea anything of the kind could possibly happen.'

'Naturally. Don't get the idea I'm putting the blame on you for what happened to Mo. Just that we have a different way of looking at things. It would never work out.'

At the doorway I took a last look at her. She was certainly the loveliest thing I ever walked out on. Maybe I should see a specialist.

'Pity,' I told her. 'You're a knockout. Well, so long, Nicola. Get rich.'

Down in the lobby there was still a struggling crowd of reporters, photographers, citizens of all kinds. They didn't notice me slipping out of the elevator and pushing into the mob. When I was near the door a tubby, breathless man grabbed me by the arm.

'Say, don't I know your face, friend? Aren't you with the Double Dee Jay show?'

He had a pencil ready to scribble down anything of interest. I looked at him sadly.

'Not me, brother. I'm just here on vacation.'

I went out into the night. The sky was the one they use on the travel folders. Ten days at a hundred a day was a thousand dollars, even by my calculations. I worked it out in bottles of scotch. If I had my figures right, by the time I emptied the last one I ought to have forgotten all about Nicola. Maybe.

We hope you have enjoyed this Large Print book. Other Chivers Press or Thorndike Press Large Print books are available at your library or directly from the publishers.

For more information about current and forthcoming titles, please call or write, without obligation, to:

Chivers Large Print
published by BBC Audiobooks Ltd
St James House, The Square
Lower Bristol Road
Bath BA2 3BH
UK
email: bbcaudiobooks@bbc.co.uk
www.bbcaudiobooks.co.uk

OR

Thorndike Press
295 Kennedy Memorial Drive
Waterville
Maine 04901
USA
www.gale.com/thorndike
www.gale.com/wheeler

All our Large Print titles are designed for easy reading, and all our books are made to last.